STEPHANIE

Stephanie, Darcy, and Allie have just opened their own baby-sitting service—and business couldn't be better. When the baby-sitters are offered a job sitting triplets at the science center, Stephanie is sure she can handle it all by herself. But she doesn't realize the triplets' parents want more than one baby-sitter for this job. And when Stephanie calls Darcy and Allie to ask for their help, they've already made other plans. If Stephanie doesn't find someone to help her with this job—fast—she'll be singing the baby-sitting blues!

MICHELLE

All right! It's Michelle's turn to baby-sit the class bunny, Al. But the first day Al is home, he eats Michelle's bag of caramels—and gets sick! Michelle has to help Al get better before the weekend is over, or she'll let her whole class down! Not to mention her Dad will never let her take care of Al again. Michelle decides her only hope is Dr. Clause, a TV veterinarian who will be appearing at the science center this weekend. But how can Michelle get Al to the science center, *and* keep her plan a secret?

FULL HOUSE™: SISTERS books

Two on the Town
One Boss Too Many
And the Winner Is . . .
How to Hide a Horse
Problems in Paradise
Will You Be My Valentine?
Let's Put On a Show
Baby-sitters & Company

Available from MINSTREL Books

For orders other than by individual consumers, Pocket Books grants a discount on the purchase of **10 or more** copies of single titles for special markets or premium use. For further details, please write to the Vice President of Special Markets, Pocket Books, 1230 Avenue of the Americas, 9th Floor, New York, NY 10020-1586.

For information on how individual consumers can place orders, please write to Mail Order Department, Simon & Schuster Inc., 100 Front Street, Riverside, NJ 08075.

Full House™ Sisters

Baby-sitters & Company

NINA ALEXANDER

A Parachute Press Book

Published by POCKET BOOKS
New York London Toronto Sydney Singapore

A MINSTREL PAPERBACK *Original*

A Minstrel Book published by
POCKET BOOKS, a division of Simon & Schuster Inc.
1230 Avenue of the Americas, New York, NY 10020

A PARACHUTE PRESS BOOK

ISBN: 0-671-04087-1

First Minstrel Books printing April 2000

10 9 8 7 6 5 4 3 2 1

Printed in the U.S.A.

STEPHANIE

Chapter 1

"Gross!" Stephanie Tanner said, wrinkling her nose. She took a head of wilting lettuce out of the refrigerator and tossed it into the trash can. *What a great way to spend Friday night,* she told herself. *Cleaning the fridge with my dad.*

Just then the phone rang. *Saved!* Stephanie thought, hopefully.

Danny Tanner held up a bunch of carrots and shook his head. "Why don't you grab that, Steph? It's probably for you—again."

"Okay." Stephanie hurried across the kitchen to pick up the phone. "Hello?"

"Hi," a woman's voice said. "May I please speak with Stephanie Tanner?"

"This is Stephanie."

"Oh, good!" the woman said. "My name is Carol Sweet, and I'm in your aunt Becky's mommy group. I understand you and your friends run a baby-sitting service. I'm looking for a good, reliable sitter for next weekend."

"Great!" Stephanie said. "You've called the right place." She carefully wrote down all the information the woman gave her. It was the third phone call she'd gotten for baby-sitting since dinner. Starting this service was the best idea Stephanie, Darcy and Allie ever had.

"Wow," Stephanie said when she rejoined her father. "Business is booming. Having Aunt Becky mention us to her mommy group was the best advertising in the world."

"That's great, Steph," Danny said. He grabbed a new sponge from under the sink. "Just don't take on more work than you can handle. That's one reason new businesses don't make it."

"Hey, it's all under control," Stephanie assured him. "We have plenty of baby-sitters to go around. Allie and Darcy are coming over tonight so we can split up the latest batch of jobs among the three of us."

Almost as soon as she finished her sentence, the doorbell rang. Stephanie checked her watch. "Oops! That's probably them now." She glanced back at the open refrigerator. There was still a lot more work to do before it would be anywhere near spotless enough for her neat-freak dad.

"Go ahead," Danny said with a smile. "I'll finish up here."

Stephanie grinned. "Thanks, Dad." Sometimes it was really handy to have a father who could read your mind—and who actually *liked* cleaning!

She hurried to answer the door. Allie and Darcy were waiting outside. "Hi, guys! Come on in."

"You'll never believe how many calls I got today," Darcy said as she walked into the house.

"Me too," Allie said. "We have jobs every weekend for the next month! We'd better figure out how booked we are before anyone else calls."

"Great," Stephanie said. "Let's get started." She led them to the couch in the living room. "We can hang out here. Michelle's taking care of her class's pet rabbit this weekend. She and her friends are up in our room playing with it."

Stephanie didn't want to admit it, but she wasn't too excited about a rabbit living in the bedroom she shared with Michelle—even if it was just for a few days. Stephanie loved pets, especially the family dog, Comet. But rabbits were different. For one thing, they smelled. They also liked to nibble on the wrong things, like phone wires or hair clips.

As if this place isn't full enough already, Stephanie thought with a smile. If they added one more person—or pet—to their household, it would burst.

Besides herself and Danny living in the house, there were Stephanie's nineteen-year-old sister, D.J., and ten-year-old sister, Michelle. Then there was Joey Gladstone, Danny's best friend. Joey had moved in years earlier to help

Danny raise Stephanie, Michelle, and D.J. after their mom died. He still lived in his apartment in the basement. Uncle Jesse moved in at the same time Joey had. Now he was married to Aunt Becky. The two of them lived on the top floor of the three-story house with their four-year-old twins, Nicky and Alex.

There's always room for one more, Stephanie thought. *Unless that one is a rabbit. . . .*

Michelle had promised to keep the bunny's cage on her side of the room and clean it out twice a day. If their room started to get stinky, Mr. Fluffy Tail was going to be *out* of there.

The girls put their papers on the coffee table and began to compare notes on the appointments they had made for the next week.

Stephanie read over her friends' lists. "Wow. We have even more jobs lined up than I thought. We've added a whole bunch since our last meeting."

"And it's mostly thanks to your aunt Becky," Darcy said. "She must have told all her friends we were the best baby-sitters in San Francisco."

Allie nodded. "Becky totally came through

for us. So we'd better get to work on our schedule. It looks like we have two new jobs for this Saturday afternoon and another one for this Saturday night."

It took a few minutes for the girls to figure out who needed to be where the next day. Then Darcy scanned the rest of the list. "We still have only two jobs for this Sunday," she pointed out. "The Myerses' kids in the evening, plus one new call—the Haverses' triplets in the afternoon."

"Triplets?" Stephanie grinned. "Hey, put me down for that one. I'm used to baby-sitting twins, remember? How much harder could triplets be?"

Allie looked doubtful. "Three little kids at once?" she said. "And all the same age? I don't know, Stephanie. Mrs. Havers said they're only four years old. Maybe we should double-team this job. I'm supposed to help out at my cousin's yard sale, but if you need me . . . ."

"Or I could skip the ball game my dad's taking me to," Darcy said reluctantly. "He isn't getting the tickets until tonight."

Stephanie bit her lip. Three little kids really did sound like a lot. But she didn't want her friends to have to cancel their plans. *I know I can do it,* she thought. *I have tons of experience with the twins.*

"Don't worry, you guys," Stephanie assured her friends. "I'm sure I can handle the Haverses' triplets on my own. Nicky and Alex are four, too. I've watched them by myself lots of times." She leaned forward on the couch and pointed at the schedule Allie was making. "And look, you guys both have tougher jobs than mine tomorrow. So I owe you."

"Are you sure?" Darcy asked. She looked worried but hopeful.

"Don't worry about it," Stephanie said, waving her hand. "I told you. I'm an expert."

Allie smiled, seeming relieved. "Okay. Thanks, Steph." She made a note on the schedule. "If you're really sure you don't need any help."

"I'm positive." Stephanie grinned. "Hey, if worse comes to worst and the triplets are hyper little monsters, all I have to do is lock all the doors and windows. That way, they can't escape from the house while I'm chasing them around and trying to keep everything under control."

Darcy laughed. "Did you ever have to do that with Nicky and Alex?"

"Nope." Stephanie winked. "Not yet. But it's always been plan B. And it's practically foolproof."

MICHELLE

Chapter 2

"What's the matter, Al?" Michelle stuck her finger through the rabbit's wire cage and poked at the carrot chunk she'd left inside. "Don't you want your snack?"

"Maybe he's full," her best friend, Cassie Wilkins, said.

"Or maybe he misses watching the fish swim around," her other best friend, Mandy Metz, suggested. "At school, their tank is right next to his cage."

Michelle sat back and studied the small brown-and-white bunny. It was Saturday morning, and her friends had come over to play with Al again. He was totally ignoring the juicy pieces of carrot she had placed right in front of his wriggling nose. "I don't know what's wrong with him today," she said, frowning. "Carrots are usually his favorite."

"No kidding. That bunny lives to eat," Mandy agreed. "When *I* brought him home, my mom joked that Al would eat anything that didn't eat him first."

Every Friday afternoon the girls' fourth-grade teacher sent Al home with a different student so he wouldn't be lonely over the weekend. This week it was Michelle's turn.

Michelle glanced at the food dish in the corner of the cage. It was still half-full of food pellets. "He didn't finish his breakfast, either," she said.

"Maybe it's too hot in this room," Cassie suggested.

Michelle brightened. "That must be it," she said, nodding. "It is pretty warm in here. And *I* never feel like eating much when I'm hot."

One of the bedroom windows was blocked by the large wire cage. Michelle hurried to the other one and pushed it up. Now fresh, cool air could flow in from outside.

She crouched down in front of the cage again. "Is that better, Al?" she asked.

The little bunny wriggled his nose at her. But he still didn't seem to notice the carrots.

"I hope he's not getting sick or something," Michelle said.

"He was fine yesterday when you brought him home," Mandy reminded her. "Maybe we wore him out by playing with him too much last night."

"I guess," Michelle said doubtfully. "But he was acting perfectly normal when I went to sleep."

"Hey, don't freak out, Michelle," Cassie said. "I'm sure it's nothing."

Michelle knew her friend was trying to make her feel better. She didn't feel better, though. She felt worried. Could something really be wrong with Al?

Maybe I should ask Dad what he thinks, Michelle thought. But she quickly scratched that idea. *No way. He didn't want me to bring a bunny home in the first place. If he thinks I'm hav-*

ing trouble taking care of Al, Dad might make me call my teacher to come and pick him up.

With a frown, Michelle remembered how much begging she had had to do before her father agreed to let Al come for a visit. *A pet is a big responsibility, Michelle,* he had lectured her. *Animals can be messy. And they take a lot of care. I'm not sure you're ready for that.*

Michelle still remembered her exact reply. *Don't worry, Dad,* she had said. *Nothing will go wrong. I promise. You won't even know Al is here.*

Michelle sighed. So far, keeping Al was fun, but it wasn't turning out to be so easy. First, Stephanie acted like sharing her room with a rabbit might poison her. And now, Al was acting funny. . . .

She stared at the bunny, wishing he would hop over and nibble on something. But he took a sip of water and then just sat motionless, staring into space. "I guess it's still too hot in here," Michelle said. "Maybe we should open the other window, too."

"I'll do it." Cassie leaned over the cage to reach the window behind it. "Hey! Can I have a piece of this candy?"

"What candy?" Michelle glanced away from Al. Her friend was holding up a bag of caramels. "Yikes!" Michelle said. "I forgot I brought those up here the other night. Dad would have a heart attack if he saw them. We're not supposed to have anything sticky or messy in our room."

"Don't worry, we won't tell." Cassie tossed the bag of candy onto Michelle's bed. She opened the window, then helped herself to a caramel. "Mmm!" she said, smiling. "These are yummy. Want one?" She held out the bag toward Michelle and Mandy.

Mandy chose a piece and popped it in her mouth. But as Michelle reached into the bag, several caramels fell out onto the floor. "Oops!" she said, bending quickly to pick them up. "There must be a hole in the bag."

"Really?" Mandy said. Her voice was slightly muffled by the sticky caramel.

"Uh-huh." Michelle checked the bag. Sure enough, she found a ragged hole, with little rips around it. They looked like tiny teeth marks.

Wait a minute, Michelle thought. She peered

into Al's cage. This time she noticed a small, crinkled piece of plastic in the wood shavings that lined the bottom of the cage. *A candy wrapper.*

"Oh, no!" Michelle cried. "The bag of caramels was on the windowsill right behind Al's cage. He must have gnawed through the plastic and sneaked some candy. *That's* why he's acting so weird! He's sick!"

What would her teacher say if the class bunny was really sick? What would all the other kids say?

I know what they'll say, Michelle thought miserably. *That I made Al sick. That it's all my fault!*

"What should I do?" she asked her friends.

Cassie shook her head. "Beats me. Maybe your dad could take you and Al to see the vet."

Michelle gulped. "But if I tell Dad, he'll find out that I wasn't responsible enough to take care of Al. I can't do that."

Mandy stuck her fingers through the cage and stroked the bunny. "You have to do *something,* Michelle," she said.

Cassie gave Michelle a sympathetic look. "If you're worried about telling your family, maybe the three of us could bring Al to the vet ourselves," she suggested. "We could take the bus. Then nobody would ever have to know."

For a second Michelle felt a surge of hope. Then she sighed. "No, that won't work, either," she said. "Our vet has been taking care of Comet since he was a puppy. She's really good friends with Dad. She'd never keep it a secret if I went to see her." Michelle began to pace the room. "Plus I'm not allowed to take the bus by myself. And how would we pay the vet, anyway? She charges a lot."

"Well, maybe we could find another vet," Cassie offered. She didn't sound very convincing. "A really cheap one who doesn't know your family and has an office that's closer . . ."

"Hey, I just remembered something!" Mandy said suddenly. "You know that TV show *Paws and Clause?"*

Michelle shrugged. "Sure," she said. *Paws and Clause* was one of her favorite shows. The host was a vet named Dr. Clause who told people how to take care of all kinds of pets. "Why? Did they do a special show on sick rabbits?"

"Nope," Mandy replied with a big grin. "Something even better. Dr. Clause is going to be appearing in person this weekend—right here in San Francisco!"

"Really?" Michelle gasped. "That means . . . if we go and see her, maybe she can help Al!"

Mandy nodded. "She's giving a talk at the Imaginarium tomorrow afternoon," she said. "I definitely remember it was Sunday because I'm supposed to go to a concert with my parents at the same time."

"The Imaginarium, huh?" Michelle rubbed her chin, thinking hard. "This plan just might work. All I have to do is find a way to get us there—right away!"

STEPHANIE

Chapter 3

Stephanie was in a great mood when she got home from her baby-sitting assignment on Saturday afternoon. As she let herself into the house, she couldn't help whistling. The job had been a breeze!

She noticed D.J. sitting on the couch. Papers and textbooks were spread across the coffee table in front of her. "Hey, D.J.!" Stephanie called.

D.J. glanced up as Stephanie tossed her jacket onto a chair. "What are *you* so cheerful about?" D.J. asked.

Stephanie noticed that her older sister

seemed a little grumpy. Checking out the mess on the coffee table, she remembered that D.J. had a big research paper due on Monday. *That explains the bad mood,* she thought.

"Oh, nothing," Stephanie answered, smiling. "I'm just the world's greatest baby-sitter, that's all. So how's the paper going?"

"Fine, I guess," D.J. said, with a small frown. She sat back on the couch and stretched. "But it's definitely going to keep me busy this weekend. I'll be lucky if I even get to sleep for the next two nights."

"Bummer," Stephanie said sympathetically.

"So, hey, what makes you the world's greatest baby-sitter?" D.J. asked.

Stephanie grinned. "I just finished watching these two little kids down the block," she said. "And they totally *loved* me. They said I was the coolest baby-sitter they'd ever had."

"That's great," D.J. said. "If they liked you that much, you'll probably get to baby-sit for them again. And the kids' parents will probably recommend you to their friends."

"I sure hope so," Stephanie said. "I can't believe what a piece of cake this baby-sitting business is!"

D.J. glanced down at her books. "Listen, Steph, I'd better get back to work."

"Okay. Good luck," Stephanie told her. She headed into the kitchen to fix herself a snack.

After she'd finished her peanut-butter-and-banana sandwich, Stephanie decided to call Mrs. Havers, the mother of the triplets she was supposed to baby-sit the next day. *I can ask if the kids have any special needs or interests,* she thought. *That way I can plan ahead.*

She pulled the Haverses' phone number out of her pocket and pressed the numbers on the keypad, feeling very professional.

"Hello?" a woman answered.

"Hello," Stephanie said politely. "This is Stephanie Tanner. May I please speak to Mrs. Havers?"

"This is she," the woman said. "Sorry, what did you say your name is again?"

Stephanie heard a commotion in the background. Mrs. Havers was probably having trouble hearing her. "It's Stephanie Tanner," she repeated more loudly. "I'm coming over tomorrow to baby-sit."

"Uh, excuse me," Mrs. Havers interrupted, sounding harried. Stephanie heard her put the phone down with a clunk. "Jack!" Mrs. Havers called. "Don't eat the cat's food. That's not for you."

Wow, Stephanie thought. *It sounds like Mrs. Havers could really use a break.*

A few moments later Mrs. Havers picked up the phone again. "Sorry about that," she said breathlessly. "Now what were you saying?"

"I was just calling to check in before I came over tomorrow," Stephanie explained patiently. "I wanted to see if there's anything special I need to know before I meet your—"

"Wait a second," Mrs. Havers interrupted. "You keep saying *I*. Shouldn't that be *we?* I thought I was hiring two girls to baby-sit tomorrow. Or was it three?"

Yikes! Stephanie thought. *She must have misunderstood when Allie explained to her about our business.*

"Um, not exactly," she said tentatively. "We thought you needed only one baby-sitter."

"Oh, no!" Mrs. Havers sounded dismayed. "I have three very young children. I really wouldn't feel comfortable leaving them with just one person—especially since I was hoping you could take them to the Imaginarium tomorrow. That's the children's museum across town."

"Yes, I know. I've been there a few times." Stephanie's mind was racing. *A trip to a museum with three little kids? That* does *sound like a lot of work.*

"I'm on the fund-raising committee at the Imaginarium," Mrs. Havers continued. "I need to put in a few hours of work in the office upstairs, but my husband is attending a big science-fiction convention that day. That means he can't watch the triplets. I was hoping you and your partner could take them around the museum for a few hours until I finish my work."

The kids' mother is going to be right there in the same building? Stephanie thought. *That'll make things tons easier. But Mrs. Havers might still decide to cancel if there is only one baby-sitter.*

"Don't worry," Stephanie told her quickly. "There will be two of us there tomorrow to take the triplets to the museum. I promise."

"Oh, good." Mrs. Havers sounded relieved. "That will be wonderful. Thank you so much."

"You're welcome." Stephanie said good-bye and hung up.

Okay, she thought, strumming her fingers on the counter. *Time to find a second baby-sitter.* She tried to remember what her friends had said they were doing on Sunday. Allie was working at a yard sale. *That probably isn't too urgent,* Stephanie thought. *I'm sure she can get out of it and come help me. Then at least Darcy won't have to miss her ball game.*

She dialed Allie's number. "Allie!" she exclaimed as soon as her friend came on the line. "Listen, I need a favor. It's about those triplets we have booked for tomorrow. I just spoke to their mom, and she practically freaked when she found out there was only one baby-sitter coming. So I told her there would be two of us. Can you do it?"

"Gosh, I'm really sorry, Stephanie," Allie said. "I can't. I decided to skip the yard sale and go visit my grandma instead. The whole family is driving up to spend the day with her. I have to go. Did you call Darcy?"

Stephanie sighed. "Not yet. I guess I'm going to have to, though."

She said good-bye, hung up, and dialed Darcy.

As soon as Stephanie started to explain the problem, Darcy cleared her throat awkwardly. "Sorry, but I can't do it, Steph," she said. "My dad got our tickets to the ball game last night. He even paid extra to get us really great seats. I can't blow him off now."

"Oh. Sure. I understand." Stephanie gulped. *Now what?*

Just don't panic, she told herself.

"Sorry," Darcy repeated. "Why don't you try Allie?"

"I already did. She can't make it, either." Stephanie chewed on her lower lip. This wasn't looking good. She needed to find another baby-sitter by tomorrow or the Havers would think she was totally irresponsible. What kind of advertising would *that* be for their business?

"So do you have any bright ideas?" she asked her friend.

"Why don't you see if D.J. could go with you?" Darcy suggested. "She's not an official employee of our baby-sitting business, but this is an emergency."

"Good idea." Stephanie felt better immediately. "D.J. has even more baby-sitting experience than I do. I'll go ask her right now." Stephanie said good-bye to Darcy and hung up.

D.J. was still sitting on the couch when Stephanie hurried into the living room. She was concentrating so hard on her work that she didn't even look up.

"Hey, D.J.," Stephanie said. "Can you do me a favor?"

"Not if it's going to take more than fifteen seconds," D.J. mumbled, without glancing up.

Stephanie gulped. D.J.'s mood seemed to be getting worse the longer she worked on her research paper. "Well," she said carefully, "*technically* it wouldn't take any time at all. Not really. I mean, you could still work on your paper. Just in a different place."

D.J. finally looked up at her. "Steph, what are you talking about?" she asked with a frown.

Stephanie grinned weakly. "Uh—want to help me baby-sit tomorrow?"

"You're kidding, right?" D.J. waved a hand at the stacks of papers, books, and index cards in front of her. "I don't even have time for this conversation. Forget baby-sitting."

"But you wouldn't have to do anything," Stephanie said quickly. "I would do all the work. Honest. I just need someone to come with me."

D.J. shook her head. "Sorry, Steph, but there's just no way." She grabbed a book from the large stack at her left elbow and started flipping through it.

Stephanie sighed. *Oh well,* she thought. *I should have guessed that D.J. wouldn't have time. But now what should I do—call Mrs. Havers back and explain?*

As soon as the thought entered Stephanie's mind, she rejected it.

No way, she told herself. *I promised Mrs. Havers that I'd show up tomorrow with a second baby-sitter. I can't let her down. It wouldn't be pro-*

fessional. I've just got *to find someone else who can come with me.*

Stephanie racked her brain as she headed upstairs. When she entered her room, her gaze fell on the big wire cage in front of the window.

The rabbit—Stephanie couldn't remember its name—seemed to be sleeping in the corner of the cage. Michelle was sitting on the edge of her bed, just staring at it. *Boy, she sure is serious about taking good care of that rabbit,* Stephanie thought. *You'd think it was a person or something.*

Then it dawned on her.

Wait a minute, Stephanie realized excitedly. The answer to her problem was sitting right in front of her: *Michelle!*

It was the perfect solution. Michelle might still be a little too young to baby-sit on her own, but she helped Stephanie watch Nicky and Alex all the time.

Michelle will love it. She always wants to tag along with me everywhere I go, Stephanie told herself. *Besides, she owes me one. I'm letting her keep her class bunny in our room all weekend. This is her chance to repay the favor.*

"Hey, Michelle," Stephanie called cheerfully. "How's it going?"

Michelle shrugged. "Okay, I guess," she muttered.

"Listen," Stephanie went on, "I've got an idea. I think you're going to like it."

"What is it?" Michelle still stared at the rabbit.

Stephanie smiled. "How would you like to come along tomorrow and help me baby-sit?"

"Tomorrow?" Michelle asked. She shook her head. "Sorry, I can't."

Stephanie blinked in surprise. "What?" she said. "Why not?"

"I just can't," Michelle repeated. "Sorry."

"Come on, Michelle," Stephanie wheedled. "It'll be easy. I'll do all the actual baby-sitting. You just get to come along and have fun."

Michelle shook her head. "Sorry. I have other stuff to do tomorrow," she said. "I really can't baby-sit with you."

Stephanie frowned, but she didn't bother to argue. She could tell by her sister's expression that she wasn't going to change her mind, no matter how much sweet-talking she did. "Okay," she said, holding up her hands and backing out of the room. "I guess it *is* kind of late notice."

Outside in the hallway, Stephanie leaned against the wall and stared into space. *So much for* that *idea,* she thought. *Now I'm really in trouble. Mrs. Havers is going to think I'm totally irresponsible. And that means, because of me, our whole baby-sitting business could go right down the tubes!*

MICHELLE

Chapter 4

Greetings, Earthling! I come in peace!"

Michelle hardly glanced at the blue two-headed alien towering over her in the hallway. "Hi, Joey," she said with a sigh.

Usually, Joey's wacky costumes and jokes made her laugh. But not today. She was too upset about Al. The bunny was looking worse than ever. And she still hadn't figured out how to get him to the Imaginarium tomorrow.

Joey pulled off his alien mask. "Hey, kiddo. Something wrong? You look kind of blue." He glanced at his mask. "Not as blue as me. But blue." He chuckled.

"Well, actually . . ." Michelle gazed at Joey. *He's goofy and fun loving,* she thought. *Just the kind of guy who might like to spend the day at a kids' museum. Maybe he'll take me.*

"I was just thinking," she said slowly. "It'd be really fun for the two of us to do something together, wouldn't it?"

"Sure, Michelle," Joey said, nodding. "That'd be great."

"Well, I have a great idea," Michelle said. "Let's go to the Imaginarium!"

Joey's eyes lit up. "The Imaginarium?" he repeated. "I *love* that place! The human-size ant tunnel exhibit is the best."

"Excellent!" Michelle gave a little leap of joy. If Joey took her to the Imaginarium, Al was saved! "How about if we go there tomorrow afternoon?"

"Tomorrow?" Joey shook his head. "Sorry, Michelle. Tomorrow is no good. I'm going to the sci-fi convention with your dad. Remember?" He held up his alien mask. "But, hey, you can come with us if you want."

Michelle felt her spirits sink again. The convention. She'd forgotten all about it. Even though Dad and Joey had been talking about it for weeks. No wonder Joey was dressed in that weird costume.

"Thanks, Joey." Michelle sighed. "But I'm not really into aliens." She wished she could tell him the whole story about why she had to go to the museum the next day. *But I can't,* she told herself miserably. *Al is totally sick—and it's all my fault. I don't want anybody to know about it.*

"Don't despair, small human," Joey said, heading off down the hall. "We'll go to your Earth museum sometime soon. Maybe next weekend." He disappeared down the stairs, practicing his scary alien laugh.

Michelle followed slowly, wandering down the stairs and entering the living room. *Okay, so Dad and Joey are definitely out,* she thought. *Who else might take me to the Imaginarium?*

She spotted D.J. sitting on the couch. Of course, D.J. loved the Imaginarium. She'd be thrilled to take her there. *I'm saved!* Michelle congratulated herself.

"Hey, D.J.," she said, hurrying over to her sister. "Want to go to the Imaginarium with me tomorrow?"

D.J. looked confused. "Huh?"

"You know, the Imaginarium," Michelle rushed on. "How about it? You and me? Tomorrow?"

D.J. gave a short laugh. "I don't think so, Michelle."

Michelle frowned. "What do you mean? Wouldn't that be fun? I really need—er, want—to go."

"Weren't you listening earlier today?" D.J. said. "You know, when I explained to everyone that I was going to be working on this stupid paper every second of the next day and a half?"

"Oops. Sorry." Michelle sighed. She had completely forgotten that. "Too bad. I really, really wanted to go to the Imaginarium with you tomorrow, D.J."

Her sister's expression grew softer. "I know, Michelle," she said kindly. "I'm sorry for snapping at you, it's just that I've got a lot on my mind right now. I'd love to go to the museum with you, too. But we'll have to do it some other time, okay?"

Some other time will be too late, Michelle thought. *I need to go tomorrow.*

Out loud, she said, "Okay, D.J. That'd be great. Good luck with your paper."

Michelle headed into the kitchen. What now? Someone just *had* to take her to the Imaginarium. Al's health depended on it!

Stephanie was leaning on the counter, talking on the phone. Michelle walked over to the refrigerator to get herself a snack. As she opened the door and started rummaging around inside, she couldn't help overhearing part of her sister's conversation.

"So I don't know what else to do, Allie," Stephanie was saying. She sounded really worried. "I mean, like I said, Mrs. Havers wants me to take the triplets to the Imaginarium, but . . ."

Michelle froze. *Am I hearing things? Or did Stephanie just mention the Imaginarium?* she wondered. She closed the refrigerator door and took a step closer to her sister.

Stephanie didn't even seem to notice her standing there. "Are you *sure* you couldn't convince your family to leave for your grandma's a little later?" she said into the phone. "I mean, I know it's kind of a long drive, but . . ."

"Steph!" Michelle whispered. She tugged on her sister's T-shirt. "I need to talk to you."

"Hold on a sec, Allie." Stephanie covered the phone with her hand. "What is it, Michelle? I'm trying to have a conversation here."

"Sorry," Michelle said. "But it's very important. I thought I just heard you say something about the Imaginarium. What are you talking about?"

Stephanie sighed. "Well, I have kind of a problem. I'm supposed to take these kids I'm baby-sitting to the museum tomorrow. But if I don't find someone to come along and help me, my baby-sitting business will be totally ruined. So now if you'll excuse me, I really have to—"

"I'll do it!" Michelle burst out. "I can help you baby-sit at the Imaginarium!"

"Really?" Stephanie asked. She sounded shocked. "Are you sure?"

"Totally sure. No problem," Michelle said. *No problem at all,* she added to herself. Now Al was as good as cured.

Stephanie uncovered the phone. "Allie? Listen, I'll have to call you back." She hung up and turned back to Michelle. "Hold on a second. I thought you had something to do tomorrow."

Michelle shrugged and grinned sheepishly. "I changed my mind. I'm in."

"All right. Now I won't have to cancel this job." Stephanie grinned and held out her hand for a high five. "Put 'er there, sister."

Michelle slapped palms with her sister. "Sure thing, sister!"

STEPHANIE

Chapter 5

Stephanie checked her watch in front of the Haverses' house. She and Michelle were a few minutes early. *Good,* she thought. *Being early was very professional.*

"Okay, here we go," she told her little sister. "Remember, it's just like I promised. You don't have to do anything at all today. *I'm* the triplets' baby-sitter. You're just coming along to make the Havers feel better."

"Got it," Michelle said. She smiled and clutched her backpack.

Stephanie glanced at the bag. "Hey, you

never did tell me exactly why you're lugging that huge thing along," she said.

"Oh, um, it's no big deal." Michelle carefully lifted the backpack onto one shoulder. "I just brought some books and stuff in case I get bored while you're baby-sitting."

"Whatever." Stephanie shrugged.

It doesn't matter if Michelle brought a whole library with her, she thought, *as long as she doesn't back out of our deal.* "Just remember," she warned her sister. "I probably won't be able to help you drag it around the museum. I'm going to have my hands full taking care of three little kids."

"Don't worry," Michelle said. "I can carry it myself."

"Good. Now let's go have some fun," Stephanie cheered. She led the way up the Haverses' walk and rang the doorbell. She could hear it jingling loudly inside the house. She could also hear the sound of loud, chattering voices and excited shrieks.

A minute or two passed. Stephanie began to wonder if anyone had heard the doorbell above all that noise. She was about to ring it again when a woman finally opened the door. She was around Aunt Becky's age, with short brown hair and wire-rimmed glasses.

"Hello," the woman said with a pleasant smile.

"Hello, Mrs. Havers," Stephanie said in her most mature, responsible voice. "I'm Stephanie Tanner, your baby-sitter. And this is my *co*-baby-sitter—my sister, Michelle." She pointed toward Michelle.

Mrs. Havers looked at Michelle and blinked. "Oh, my," she said, sounding surprised. "How old are you, dear?"

"She's ten, Mrs. Havers," Stephanie jumped in before her sister could answer. "I know she might be a little younger than you were expecting, but let me assure you, Michelle has a *lot* of baby-sitting experience. She helps me watch our aunt and uncle's four-year-old twins all the time."

"Really?" the woman pushed her glasses up higher on her nose. "Michelle, do you watch Becky's twins?"

That's right, Stephanie remembered. *Mrs. Havers belongs to Aunt Becky's mommy group. That's how she knows her first name.*

"Yes," Michelle answered. "I watch Nicky and Alex all the time."

Mrs. Havers stared at Michelle for a moment, then she sighed. "Well, all right, then," she said. "If Becky trusts you, then I certainly do, too. Why don't you girls come in and meet the triplets?"

Stephanie heaved a silent sigh of relief. *Whew,* she thought. *I never even imagined that Mrs. Havers might think Michelle was too young. But I'm glad she trusts us.*

Mrs. Havers led Stephanie and Michelle into a large room off the main hallway. There wasn't much furniture in the room, except for a couch and a cabinet that held a TV set. Toys were scattered everywhere. Two little boys and a little girl were playing on the carpet near the couch.

All of the kids had brown hair the same shade as their mother's. One of the boys had curly hair and the other's was straight. Their sister's hair was gathered into two short braids.

They're so cute, Stephanie thought, smiling. *I like them already.*

"Look who's here, everybody," Mrs. Havers said brightly. "It's your new baby-sitters! This is Stephanie, and this is Michelle. And guess what? They're sisters."

"Sisters are dumb," the curly-haired boy said, giggling. He poked the little girl in the shoulder.

She stuck out her tongue at him. "We are *not!"*

"Okay, that's enough." Mrs. Havers told the triplets. She shot Stephanie and Michelle an apologetic glance. "Sorry, but I guess you know how siblings are," she said. "They love to tease each other."

"Oh, yeah, we know all about that," Stephanie said. She nudged Michelle playfully. "Right, sis?"

"What? Oh, um, yeah," Michelle said.

Stephanie raised one eyebrow at Michelle. Her sister seemed a little distracted. She was *supposed* to be making a good impression on Mrs. Havers. *What's on Michelle's mind?* Stephanie wondered.

Luckily, Mrs. Havers didn't seem to notice. She smiled fondly at the triplets. "All right, then," she said. She pointed to the curly-haired boy, then the straight-haired one. "That's Jack, and that's Jimmy, and their sister's name is Janie."

"Jack, Jimmy, Janie," Stephanie repeated, memorizing which kid was which. "That's easy. Got it."

"Good." Mrs. Havers checked her watch. "I guess I'll leave you all for a few minutes to get acquainted. I have to finish getting my papers together before we go." She bent down and patted Jimmy on the shoulder. "Be good, sweeties. I'll be right back."

As soon as Mrs. Havers was out of the room, Stephanie turned to the triplets and gave them a big, friendly smile. "Hi there!" she said. "My name's Stephanie."

"We know that already," the little girl piped up. "Mommy just told us. You're Steph'nie, and she's Michelle."

"That's right." Stephanie nodded. "You're very smart, Janie."

"Yeah, she's a big smarty-pants," Jimmy

put in. He was playing with a puppy-shaped wooden puzzle.

Jack giggled. "Smarty-pants! Smarty-pants!" he teased.

Janie scowled at her brothers. "Oh, yeah?" she said. "Well, you're dumb! Dumb-dumb! Dumb-dumb!" She turned it into a song, doing her best to drown out Jack, who continued his smarty-pants chant.

Stephanie smiled uncertainly. The triplets sure were lively. Still, they were no worse than a lot of the other kids she baby-sat for. "Okay," she told them firmly. "No name-calling. It's not nice."

The three kids were instantly silent. *Cool,* Stephanie thought. *They totally listened to me!*

"Hey, Steph'nie," Jimmy said. "Are we going to see animals at the . . . um . . ." He hesitated, looking helpless.

" 'Mag-nar-um," Janie said. "That's the name of the museum. Right, Steph'nie?"

"Almost right!" Stephanie said brightly. "It's called the Imaginarium, and it's a really, really fun place. And, sure, I bet we'll see lots of animal exhibits while we're there."

"Yay!" Jimmy cheered.

Stephanie shot a quick glance at her sister. *I hope Michelle is paying attention,* she thought. *She could pick up some tips from me in case she wants to do some baby-sitting when she gets older. You just have to know how to talk to kids.*

But Michelle wasn't paying any attention at all. She was perched on the edge of the couch with her backpack on her lap. Her gaze seemed to be fixed on the top zipper of the bag.

Stephanie shrugged. *Maybe Michelle didn't get enough sleep last night,* she thought. *She is totally out of it today.*

Stephanie turned back to the triplets. "So, besides animals, what else do you want to see at the Imaginarium?" she asked them.

"Animals!" Jimmy shouted. He started jumping up and down so much that he knocked over a nearby stack of picture books. "Animals! Animals!"

Stephanie winced. For such a young kid, Jimmy sure had a loud voice. "Okay, Jimmy," she said patiently. "We already talked about the animals. But there are other interesting things to see at the museum, too."

Jimmy looked stubborn. "Animals!" he yelled once more. This time he was so loud that even Michelle looked at him and frowned slightly.

"He likes animals a lot," Janie explained. She stuck the end of one braid in her mouth.

Stephanie chuckled. "I can see that, Janie."

"I'm hungry," Jack announced suddenly. He stood up and marched toward the door at the back of the room.

Beyond the doorway, Stephanie could see a kitchen. "Wait!" she said, hurrying after Jack and almost tripping over a toy piano. "Um, are you *sure* you're hungry?"

"Jack's always hungry," Janie answered for her brother. "He eats and eats and eats and eats and—"

"I see," Stephanie broke in. "But I'm not sure your mom would want him to—"

Just then Mrs. Havers walked into the room. "Everybody ready to go?" she asked.

Good, Stephanie thought, relieved at the interruption. *It's time to get to the Imaginarium and get this baby-sitting job started for real.*

"We're ready," she reported. "Right kids? Let's go!"

"Wait a minute," Mrs. Havers said. She was looking at Janie's feet. Janie's *stockinged* feet. "Young lady," Mrs. Havers said sternly, "what did you do with your shoes?"

Stephanie felt herself blush. *Oops,* she thought. *I really should have noticed she only had socks on.*

Luckily Mrs. Havers didn't seem too concerned. "You have to watch Janie like a hawk," she explained to Stephanie. "She hates wearing shoes. She'll take them off and hide them whenever she thinks she can get away with it."

"Oh," Stephanie said meekly. "Um, Michelle and I will help you find them. Come on, Michelle."

She thought she caught her little sister rolling her eyes, but Michelle got up and joined the search. Before long, Stephanie found one small shoe stuffed under the couch. Mrs. Havers located the other behind a pile of alphabet blocks.

"All right, sweetie," Mrs. Havers said. She

took both shoes and set them down in front of Janie. "Let's get these back on so you can go around the nice museum with your new baby-sitters, okay?"

"No," Janie said stubbornly. "My feet are hot."

"Janie . . ." Mrs. Havers began.

It's time to start earning my baby-sitting fee, Stephanie decided. "Hey, Janie," she said cheerfully. "I've got a joke for you. What do you get when you cross a cow with a duck?"

Janie looked interested. "What?"

Stephanie waggled her finger and smiled. "I'll only tell you if you let your mommy put your shoes back on."

Janie frowned. For a second Stephanie was afraid the little girl wasn't going to fall for it. But then Janie pointed to her shoes. "Mommy!" she said. "Shoes! Hurry!"

"All right," Mrs. Havers said, tiredly. "Sit still, sweetie."

"So," Stephanie said when Janie's shoes were back on her feet. "*Now* do you want to know what you get when you cross a cow with a duck?" She grinned. "Milk and quackers!"

Janie laughed with delight. Mrs. Havers shot Stephanie a grateful look.

Cool, Stephanie thought. *That joke was always one of my personal faves from Joey's old comedy act. I'll have to remember to tell him that it's still a big hit—with four-year-olds, anyway.*

Mrs. Havers led them all out of the house and onto the front stoop. "Oh, good. My husband brought the car around already. That's him right there, in the blue minivan." She pointed to a vehicle idling at the curb. "Why don't you girls take the kids down and help him strap them in? I'll lock up."

"Sure thing, Mrs. Havers." Stephanie took Jimmy by one hand and Jack by the other. "Michelle," she called, "grab Janie, would you?"

Michelle took the little girl's hand. Everyone marched down the sidewalk toward the curb.

As they approached the minivan, a tall man with thinning dark hair jumped out of the driver's seat.

"Hi, there!" he said, with a friendly smile. "I'm the father of this wacky bunch. You must be the new baby-sitters."

"That's us." Stephanie introduced herself and Michelle to Mr. Havers. "So where should everyone sit?"

Mr. Havers scratched his head. "Well, let's see now. The triplets' car seats pretty much take up the whole middle seat. So that means you girls are way in the back."

Stephanie looked at the rear seat of the minivan. It was almost completely covered with toys. Ugh.

"Sounds great," she said.

"Okay, then." Mr. Havers smiled at her. "Let's get these guys strapped in."

It took a while, but Stephanie and the Havers finally managed to get the triplets safely buckled into their car seats.

"Okay," Mrs. Havers said, climbing into her own seat. "Jimmy, do you have your Bubba Bear? Jack, here's a cracker. Janie, why don't you look at this nice book during the ride?" Mrs. Havers passed out the appropriate item to each child. "All right," she said at last, sounding exhausted. "I think we're ready to go."

Mr. Havers opened the rear gate of the van. "In you go, girls," he said.

Stephanie hopped in. "Come on, Michelle," she said. "Hurry up."

"I'm coming." Michelle was cradling her backpack again. She seemed to be taking special care not to bump it as she climbed into the backseat of the minivan.

Stephanie bit her lip. *Since when is Michelle so cautious about getting in a car?* she wondered. "Do you need some help, Michelle?" she asked. She reached out and grabbed the backpack.

Michelle gasped, and shoved Stephanie's hand away. "Hey, don't squash it."

"Sorry." Stephanie wrinkled her brow. "I was just trying to help." She glanced toward the front of the van. Luckily, the Havers weren't paying attention to them at all.

Finally Michelle was settled with her backpack on her lap. Mr. Havers started the car. "We're off," he called cheerfully.

"Yay!" Jimmy yelled. "We're going to see the animals!"

"I want to see the fake volcano," Janie said. "Mommy said I could."

Jack pounded his fists on his car seat. "No!" he cried. "Snack first!"

"Oh, that reminds me," Mrs. Havers called to Stephanie and Michelle. "I want to give you girls some money for food." She twisted around in her seat and passed a twenty-dollar bill back to Stephanie. "Don't let Jack eat everyone's snack, okay?" She winked.

"Snack!" Jack shouted. "Snack! I want a snack *now!"*

"Let's sing the snack song!" Jimmy suggested.

"Yeah!" Janie and Jack cried.

The triplets suddenly started singing at the top of their lungs. The tune was the same as "Twinkle, Twinkle, Little Star." But instead of the regular words, the Havers kids just sang "Snack, snack, snack, snack, snack, snack, snack!"

Stephanie felt like sticking her fingers in her ears. Or better yet, jumping out of the car at the next red light. *What's with these kids?* she wondered. *They're so . . .* loud! Then she realized they weren't really any louder than other kids their age—there were just more of them.

And they're probably just overexcited about the trip to the Imaginarium, Stephanie told herself.

Maybe when we get there they'll calm down a little. At least I hope so.

Finally Mr. Havers pulled up to the curb in front of the museum. "Everybody out that's getting out," he said.

Unloading the triplets from the car turned out to be a lot quicker and easier than loading them in. Mrs. Havers kissed Mr. Havers good-bye, and everyone waved as he drove off.

Then Mrs. Havers led the way into the museum. "Okay, folks," she said, checking her watch. "I'm going to head upstairs now. Kids, you have fun. Do exactly what Stephanie and Michelle say, all right?"

"Don't worry, Mrs. Havers," Stephanie said. "We're going to have a blast. Right, kids?"

The triplets cheered, and Mrs. Havers smiled. "Good," she said. "I'll meet you right back here in front of this horse statue at four o'clock. Okay?"

"You've got it," Stephanie told her.

Mrs. Havers waved and hurried toward a marble staircase at the rear of the lobby.

The triplets called good-bye until their mother disappeared from sight. Then

Stephanie motioned for them to follow her across the crowded lobby toward the museum directory. "This way, everyone!" she sang out. "Let's decide what we want to see first."

"Uh, Steph?" Michelle scrambled to catch up. "I don't think they heard you."

Stephanie turned around and gasped. The triplets had sped off in three different directions. "Jack! Jimmy! Janie!" she cried. "Wait!"

MICHELLE

Chapter 6

It's a good thing little kids can't run that fast, Michelle thought as she helped Stephanie round up the triplets. *Otherwise, this baby-sitting job would be over before it began.*

Once everyone was safely back in a group, Michelle gazed around the museum lobby. It was three stories high, with a shiny marble floor and whitewashed walls. Huge colorful banners decorated the walls, advertising the special exhibits.

There! Michelle saw what she was looking for: a purple banner with a picture of a cat and a dog on it. Above the picture was the logo for

Paws and Clause, Dr. Clause's show. Michelle patted her backpack gently and smiled. Soon she would know exactly what was wrong with Al and how to make him better.

Just then someone bumped into her. Michelle turned quickly, protecting her bag. "Sorry," a boy said, hurrying off.

Michelle sighed. By now crowds of kids and parents were hurrying in and out of the museum. It looked like the Imaginarium was going to be pretty crowded.

I forgot how big this place is, Michelle thought. *I hope Cassie and I don't have any trouble finding each other.*

She and Cassie had arranged for Cassie's parents to drop her off on the way to a wedding. Michelle gulped. For the first time, she realized that the Havers would have to drive Cassie back to the Tanners' house. *I hope they won't have a problem with that,* she thought.

Michelle looked over at her sister. *I hope Stephanie doesn't have a problem with it, either,* she added to herself. *Maybe I should have mentioned that Cassie was coming to meet me here.*

It looked like Stephanie had her hands full

at the moment. The triplets were playing tag, chasing one another in circles around Stephanie and the directory sign. They were giggling and shrieking loudly. Stephanie waved her arms at all three of them, begging them to settle down.

Maybe I'll tell her about Cassie later, Michelle thought.

She glanced at her backpack. She hoped that Al was okay inside. She kept trying to peek in to check on him, but it was hard to do that without looking suspicious. She eased the zipper open a bit more to give the bunny more air. Then she made sure she was far enough away from the hyper triplets. She didn't want them to bump into Al while they were horsing around.

Michelle stepped over to check out the directory. A colorful sign was posted next to the map of the museum. Michelle smiled as she read:

Dr. Clause films an episode of
Paws and Clause
Today!
At the Imaginarium Rotunda!
3 P.M.

All right, Michelle thought eagerly. *The vet really is here today.* "Hang in there," she whispered to the bunny in her bag. "Everything's going to be okay."

She checked her watch. It was only a little after one o'clock. The taping wasn't for another two hours. That left plenty of time for her to find Cassie and then track down Dr. Clause before the taping started.

It would be better to talk to the vet then, Michelle decided. Dr. Clause would probably be too busy during the taping.

"Hey," a familiar voice called. "Michelle."

Michelle turned and saw Cassie hurrying toward her.

"Hey," Michelle said. She waved at Cassie's mother, who waved back and then hurried toward the exit.

"Cassie?" Stephanie came over after rebuckling one of Janie's shoes. She blinked at Michelle's friend in surprise. "What are *you* doing here? Did Michelle tell you we were coming today?"

"Um, I guess I might have mentioned it," Michelle said quickly. She gave a weak laugh.

Stephanie looked confused, but Jack and Jimmy were both tugging on her arms. While her sister was distracted, Michelle grabbed Cassie and pulled her aside. "Did you see the sign?"

"Uh-huh." Cassie nodded. "I even went to the information booth and asked for a map so we could find the Rotunda." She pulled a pamphlet out of her pocket and unfolded it, revealing a floor plan of the entire museum.

Michelle scanned the map. "Okay," she said. "It looks like we need to go up the west stairway. The Rotunda is just past the Hall of Dinosaurs. Once we get there, all we have to do is start asking people where Dr. Clause is. Once she sees Al, she'll definitely agree to talk to us."

"Sounds like a plan." Cassie glanced at Michelle's backpack. "Is Al in there?" she whispered. "How is he doing?"

"I'm not sure," Michelle admitted. "He was sleeping when it was time to leave. I just stuck him in there with a towel to sleep on and a few carrots in case he changes his mind about eating."

She turned to check on the others. Stephanie was peering at the signs pointing to different exhibits, trying to hold on to all three excited kids at the same time.

"Settle down, guys, okay?" Stephanie told them. "Please, we can see everything you want. But only one exhibit at a time. Let's start with the animals."

"Hey, I have an even better idea," Michelle spoke up. "Why don't we go to the Hall of Dinosaurs."

Once we're there, she thought, *it will be a piece of cake for me and Cassie to sneak over to the Rotunda right next door. Then we can find Dr. Clause—and find out how to help Al.*

"Yeah," Janie cried, jumping up and down. "Hall of Dinosaurs!"

"No, animals!" Jimmy cried. "I want to see the animals."

Jack grinned. "I vote for animals. We win!"

Janie began to cry. "Michelle said we could go to the dinosaurs."

Stephanie knelt down in front of the little girl. "Don't cry, Janie," she said. "We'll spend extra time in the Hall of Dinosaurs later, okay?" She glared at Michelle.

Michelle felt terrible. She couldn't really blame Stephanie for being annoyed with her.

I didn't mean to cause trouble, Michelle thought. *But I've got other things to worry about right now. Al is depending on me.*

Her gaze wandered to her backpack. She wondered if the bunny was comfortable enough. He still hadn't been acting like his usual friendly self that morning. In fact, Michelle thought he looked sicker than ever.

"Okay!" Stephanie clapped her hands. "So we'll go to see the animals first and the dinosaurs later. Agreed?" The kids nodded. Stephanie glanced around at the arrows on the walls pointing to different exhibits. *Animals, Animals, Animals* pointed off to the left. "Come on, guys. This way."

"It's okay if I tag along, right?" Cassie said.

"Is it, Stephanie?" Michelle asked. "Please?"

Stephanie shrugged. "It's fine with me, I guess," she said. "Just remember, I have a job to do. So I really can't watch you two and take care of the triplets."

Michelle rolled her eyes at Cassie. "Don't worry, Steph. We can take care of ourselves." Sometimes it was hard being the youngest sister.

"Okay," she whispered to Cassie a few minutes later as the entire group headed toward the entrance to *Animals, Animals, Animals.* "How are we going to get everyone to the Hall of Dinosaurs—or anywhere else near the Rotunda? We're going in the opposite direction right now. And who knows how long it will take us to track down Dr. Clause? We don't want to waste any time."

"I know," Cassie said. She pointed at Stephanie, who was trying to keep up as the triplets raced ahead. "But maybe they won't want to stay in the animal exhibit very long."

"Are you *kidding?* Didn't you hear Jimmy? That kid is crazy about animals." Michelle looked at Jimmy. Suddenly she had an idea. "Hey, Steph," she said, hurrying after her sister. "I was just thinking, maybe we should play a game while we're looking. How about hide-and-seek? We could all hide around the museum and you could come and find us."

"Yeah!" Janie cried. "Hide-and-seek!"

Stephanie stared at Michelle in stunned disbelief. "You're kidding, right? You don't really think I'm going to let the triplets run around the museum without me, do you? Michelle, what if they get lost? Or hurt?"

Michelle gulped. Her sister had a point. *I guess hide-and-seek in the museum isn't exactly the best idea I've ever had,* Michelle thought.

"We won't get hurt. I want to play," Jack said.

"Hide-and-seek! Hide-and-seek!" the boys chanted together.

"Um, Michelle?" Stephanie said, trying to smile. "Remember what we talked about earlier? You know, about me being the head baby-sitter and all that?"

"Sorry." Michelle shrugged. "I wasn't thinking." She sighed and rejoined Cassie. "I guess we're stuck with the animals for now," she told her friend.

She and Cassie followed Stephanie and the triplets into *Animals, Animals, Animals.* As usual, Jimmy, Janie, and Jack started yelling at the top of their lungs about the exhibit the moment they stepped into it.

"Isn't this fun?" Stephanie asked the triplets through clenched teeth. "Now we all have to stay together or we won't get to see everything."

Michelle sank down onto a bench facing a life-size diorama of a rain forest.

Cassie sat beside her. "Hey, it's pretty dark in here," she said. "Why don't we take Al out for a second and make sure he's okay?"

"Good idea." Michelle glanced around. Cassie was right. The room was very dim so that people could see the brightly lit exhibits better. *Who's going to notice a little brown-and- white bunny?* Michelle asked herself. *Especially if we took him out only for a minute or two.*

She unzipped her backpack and reached inside. Then she lifted the furry animal from the bottom of the bag. When she pulled Al out, he wriggled slightly for a moment. Then he stopped and hung limply from Michelle's hands.

"Yikes! He looks worse than ever," Cassie cried. Then she caught herself and slapped her hand to her mouth. "Sorry, Michelle."

Michelle stroked the rabbit softly on his head. Poor Al. He *did* look terrible. Tears pricked her eyes. "We have to find Dr. Clause now," she told Cassie. "Before it's too late."

"Well, she must be over near the Rotunda somewhere," Cassie said. She sighed. "But how can we get over there if we're stuck with your sister?"

"I don't know," Michelle said grimly. "But we'll figure out a plan—soon. I'm going to make sure Dr. Clause sees Al. No matter what it takes!"

STEPHANIE

Chapter 7

"Hold on, Jimmy!" Stephanie called. She dropped Janie's hand and raced forward just in time to stop Jimmy from wandering ahead into the next part of the exhibit, an Australian scene. "We have to stay together, remember?"

Jimmy pointed ahead. "But I want to see the kangaroos," he complained.

Jack was pulling at the leg of her pants, singing the snack song again. Stephanie felt totally frazzled. *Wow!* she thought. *Taking care of triplets is no joke.*

She glanced back at her little sister. Michelle and Cassie were still sitting on a bench near the entrance to the exhibit. They seemed to be peering into Michelle's backpack.

Stephanie shook her head, thinking about Michelle's suggestions today. Four-year-olds playing hide-and-seek in a museum? Boy, Michelle sure had a lot to learn about baby-sitting. She knew Michelle was just trying to be helpful. But so far, her ideas had been pretty useless.

Oh well, Stephanie thought. *I did tell her I'd handle everything myself. At least having Michelle and Cassie along is better than being all alone.*

She turned her attention back to the triplets. Jimmy was still trying to wriggle out of her grip. Janie was sitting on the edge of an exhibit platform, yanking at her left shoe.

"Janie!" Stephanie cried. "Wait, leave that on."

Janie pouted. "My feet are hot!" she complained. But she stopped fiddling with her buckle and stood up.

Stephanie glanced around. *Where's Jack?* she wondered, frowning. She soon spotted him standing nearby. He was staring hungrily at a toddler's lollipop.

"Jack!" Dropping Jimmy's hand, Stephanie hurried over and gently pulled him away. "Come on, now. It's not nice to take other people's snacks!"

Jack scowled. "I'm hungry!"

"I know, and I'm sorry." Stephanie patted him on the shoulder. "But you can't go around drooling on other kids' food. What would your parents say?"

Jack smiled, his cheeks forming matching dimples. "They would say, Give me a snack!"

Stephanie couldn't help laughing. "Nice try."

She looked over her shoulder. Now Janie was wandering into the Australia exhibit. She guessed Jimmy was already there, looking at the kangaroos.

"Yo!" she called to Michelle and Cassie. "We're moving on, guys." Taking Jack by the hand, she hurried into the next room.

When she got there, she spotted Jimmy right away. The Australia room wasn't very crowded. The little boy was planted right in front of the main exhibit. He was gazing at it in awe.

Stephanie didn't blame him. The exhibit was pretty cool. It was raised up on a low platform that looked exactly like a reddish desert floor. The lighting was low, making it feel like nighttime.

Life-size sculpted models of grazing kangaroos were scattered across the fake desert. Among them were several other strange-looking animals and birds.

Nearby was a replica of a native Australian camp. The natives were sitting by a campfire, playing long, unusual-looking instruments painted with colorful designs.

"Listen to this, kids," Stephanie said, scanning the sign in front of the exhibit. "It says here that more than a hundred artists worked on this scene for a whole year." She read on, impressed by all the details. "The museum flew in expert scientists from Australia to help," she told Jack. The little boy was still clinging to her hand as he gazed at the desert scene, sucking on the fingers of his other hand. "Some of the things up there are very valuable. In fact, it says here the whole exhibit cost more than a million . . ."

Janie's squeal interrupted her. "Look, Steph'nie! Jimmy's a kangaroo!"

Stephanie gasped. Jimmy had climbed onto the raised floor of the exhibit. "Jimmy!" she cried. "Get down from there! Right now!"

Jimmy didn't seem to hear her. He was walking across the fake desert floor, giggling loudly. He looked very pleased with himself. "I'm a kangaroo!" he cried, hopping up and down.

He stopped to pat one of the model kangaroos on the head. Stephanie could see the fake animal wobbling beneath the little boy's enthusiastic pats.

She glanced around. *Oh, no!* The other museum visitors in the room were starting to notice what Jimmy was doing. *I've got to get him down from there before he breaks something—like one of those priceless artifacts,* Stephanie thought frantically.

"Jimmy!" she called. But she was afraid to yell too loudly. There was a security guard standing at the far end of the room. She noticed he was facing the other way right then.

Michelle and Cassie came up to her.

"Uhh—Steph," Michelle said. "I don't think he's supposed to be walking around up there."

"No kidding," Stephanie exclaimed. "I've got to get him down before he gets us kicked out of the museum!"

"Look," Jack said happily. "Jimmy's going to hop right into those people in the funny costumes."

Stephanie cringed as Jimmy kangaroo-hopped closer to the native camp—the part of the exhibit with the priceless artifacts.

"You two stay right here with Michelle," she told Jack and Janie firmly.

Taking a deep breath, she hopped up onto the exhibit herself. Her shoes crunched on the fake desert sand. She hurried toward Jimmy, being careful not to bump into anything.

"Jimmy!" she called softly. "Hey, wait up!"

The little boy laughed. "No way! I'm a kangaroo. You can't catch me."

He hopped away, almost crashing into one of the native models. Stephanie gasped in horror, then dove after him. She had to grab him before it was too late!

Her hand closed around a handful of Jimmy's T-shirt. "Gotcha," she cried.

Jimmy shrieked and twisted away. Stephanie felt the fabric slipping through her grasp. *Oh, no, you don't,* she thought, lunging forward again.

In midleap she felt something hold her back. "Uh-oh," she muttered, afraid to turn her head. Was it a museum guard?

No such luck. Behind her was one of the fake native Australians, standing near the campfire. The model was holding some kind of long, pointy weapon. Stephanie's shirt was stuck on it.

"Oh, no!" she groaned. She tried to reach back and free herself. But her arm wouldn't stretch far enough. And when she made a move to pull away, the fake man teetered dangerously. If she yanked her shirt free, he might topple over and break.

Now what am I going to do? Stephanie wondered. She glanced desperately back toward the viewing area. Michelle was holding Jack's hand, and Cassie was holding Janie's. Meanwhile, Jimmy was still hopping around the exhibit. Both Michelle and Cassie looked as if they were going to burst out laughing.

"Great," Stephanie muttered to herself. "Just great."

"Michelle!" she called. "Help! I'm stuck!"

In response, her little sister lost it. Totally. In fact, she was laughing so hard that she was practically doubled over, grabbing her stomach.

How embarrassing! Stephanie felt her face turn red. "Michelle!" she snapped. "This isn't funny!"

"I—I know," Michelle gasped out, still cracking up. Cassie was laughing, too. Even some of the other museum visitors were smiling at her predicament.

Things couldn't possibly get any worse, Stephanie thought. Then she saw something that made her heart stop. *Oh, no!* she thought. *I guess things can get worse.* She froze in place. The museum security guard was coming right toward her!

MICHELLE

Chapter 8

"Michelle, we have to help your sister get unstuck," Cassie insisted. "If the guard catches her up there, he'll probably kick us *all* out of the museum. Then we'll never get to see Dr. Clause!"

Michelle's giggles immediately faded. *Cassie's right,* she thought. *I have to help Stephanie.* She glanced over her shoulder and gasped. "Uh-oh," she whispered to Cassie. "It's too late."

A museum security guard was heading straight for Stephanie. He was a big, burly man with a reddish-brown mustache and curly hair. He wore a dark-green uniform and matching hat.

Michelle gave Cassie Jack's hand. Then she set her backpack carefully on the floor beside her friend. "Watch that, okay?" she instructed.

She hurried over to the guard. "Excuse me," she said. She grabbed his uniform sleeve. "That's my sister up there. She didn't mean to wreck the exhibit or anything. Really. She was just chasing one of the kids she—er, *we*—are baby-sitting."

The guard raised an eyebrow. "Is that right?" he replied. "Well, I'd better get them both down before someone gets hurt or something gets broken."

Michelle stood back and crossed her fingers. *He didn't sound too mad,* she thought. *Maybe we won't get kicked out after all.*

Cassie picked up Michelle's backpack and came over to join her. Jack and Janie trailed behind. "What do you think?" Cassie asked. "Are we in trouble?"

Michelle shook her head. "It's hard to tell," she said.

They watched as the guard headed toward Jimmy. The little boy was crouched down examining a baby kangaroo. "Just stay still for a second, miss," the guard called over his shoulder to Stephanie.

"He seems pretty nice," Cassie whispered to Michelle. "Maybe we'll be lucky."

"Hi," Jimmy said to the guard. "You're taller than my daddy. Are you a giant?"

The guard smiled. "Not quite, son," he said. "Now why don't you come with me? There are lots of other things to see in the museum, you know."

Jimmy thought about that. "More animals?" he asked.

"Lots more." The guard nodded.

"Okay," Jimmy agreed. He jumped up. "Animals are my favorite!"

Taking the little boy by the hand, the guard carefully led him off the platform. Then he brought him over to Michelle. "You'd better hang on to this one extra-tight, young lady," he said, smiling. "I'm going to see if I can rescue your sister now."

"Okay," Michelle said. "I mean, yes, sir. Thanks." She took Jimmy's hand.

Jimmy wriggled, trying to break her grasp. "Come on!" he cried. "The giant said there were more animals!"

Michelle held on, but it was hard to keep her grip on Jimmy and keep an eye on the other two kids at the same time. She had to do something—fast!

"Hey, Jimmy." She gave the little boy a bright smile. "How about this? If you stand still for just a few minutes, I'll give you a whole dollar. Then you can buy yourself some animal stuff in the gift shop. Okay?"

Jimmy instantly stopped squirming. "Really?" he said. "Okay! I'll stand totally still, Michelle." He froze like a statue.

"That's great," Michelle said.

"Michelle! Michelle!" Janie tugged on Michelle's sleeve. "What about *me?* I've been standing still this whole time. Can I have a dollar, too?"

"Me, too! Me, too!" Jack cried. "I want to buy snacks."

Michelle bit her lip. What could she do?

"Cassie," she whispered. "Do you have a dollar I can borrow? I only have two bucks left from my allowance."

"Sure," Cassie whispered back. "My mom gave me some money for the museum." She dug a dollar bill out of her jeans and handed it over.

Michelle shot her a grateful smile. "Thanks." She tucked the money in her own pocket. Cassie was an awesome friend.

"Okay," she told the kids. "You can each have a dollar to spend on whatever you want. But only if you're all very, *very* good for the next few minutes. Got it?"

The triplets nodded eagerly.

Michelle turned back to see what was happening to her sister. By now, at least a dozen people were gawking at Stephanie and whispering.

Yikes, Michelle thought. *Poor Steph. I bet nothing like this ever happened on any of her babysitting jobs before.*

Stephanie grinned weakly as the guard approached her. "Uh, hello, sir," she began loudly. "I'm really, *really* sorry about this.

Jimmy just gets really excited about animals. I guess I took my eyes off him for, like, a split second, and—"

"I understand, miss," the guard said kindly. "It could happen to anyone." He carefully detached Stephanie's shirt from the pointy weapon. Then he led her off the exhibit.

"He's not mad," Michelle whispered to Cassie. "*Whew!*"

Even in the dim lighting, Michelle could see that her sister's face was beet-red. "Thanks," Stephanie told the guard. "And I really am sorry. It won't happen again."

The guard gave Stephanie a little salute. "No problem. Just try to keep a better grip on the little guy from now on, okay?"

"I sure will," Stephanie replied quickly.

The guard walked away, and Stephanie rejoined the group. "Well," she said, smoothing her shirt. "*That* was a close call."

"Don't worry," Michelle told her sister. She really wanted to make Stephanie feel better. "Cassie and I took good care of the triplets while you were up there. We even got them to stand still. See?" She pointed to Jack, Jimmy, and Janie. The kids were standing perfectly frozen.

"Wow." Stephanie raised her eyebrows. "Pretty good, Michelle. So what's your secret?"

"She said we could have a dollar!" Jack burst out.

Stephanie frowned. "Michelle! You didn't really promise them money, did you?"

"Yes, she did!" Janie spoke up. "We're going to be rich!"

Michelle gulped. Stephanie suddenly looked a lot less happy, but a promise was a promise. "Um, here you go, kids," she said. She pulled out the three dollar bills and handed them out to the triplets. "Good job, guys."

Stephanie glared at her. *"Michelle,"* she began through clenched teeth.

Boy, is she annoyed, Michelle thought. *Time to get out of here—fast!*

"Uhh—come on, Cassie," she said quickly. "Let's go see what's in the next room, okay?" She moved toward the door.

"Sure." Cassie followed Michelle. Stephanie didn't say a word to stop them. She was too busy explaining to the kids why they had to be good even when they weren't getting paid.

On the way out of the Australia room, Michelle spotted the friendly guard. "Hey, Cassie," she whispered, nudging her friend. "I've got an idea."

"What?" Cassie whispered back.

"Why don't we ask that nice guard about Dr. Clause? Maybe he knows where she's going to be before the taping."

Cassie nodded. "Great idea, Michelle. The sooner we can find her, the better." She patted Michelle's backpack, which she was still carrying. "Hang in there, Al!"

Michelle took a deep breath and went over to the guard. She tapped him on the arm. "Excuse me."

The guard looked down and grinned when he recognized her. "Well, if it isn't the baby-sitters," he said in a jolly tone. "What happened? Did you lose another one?"

Michelle smiled. "Um, no," she said. "We just have a question for you."

"Well, that's what I'm here for, young lady," the guard said. "Ask away."

"It's about Dr. Clause," Cassie spoke up eagerly. "Do you know when she's getting here?"

The guard scratched his chin. "Well, the taping begins at three." He checked his watch. "That's more than an hour away. You girls still have plenty of time to enjoy the museum before you need to head over to the Rotunda."

"No," Michelle blurted out. She stopped herself. "Um, I mean, we know that. What we were really wondering is if Dr. Clause is at the museum yet."

"Oh, I see." The guard nodded. "Yes, I happen to know that she is in the building. I saw her myself a little while ago. But right now she's probably backstage, getting ready for her show. No one is allowed back there except authorized personnel. So you'll just have to be patient and wait until three o'clock."

"But we—" Cassie began.

Michelle nudged her. She didn't want her friend to give away their plan. "Thank you," she said loudly, cutting off her friend in midsentence. "Thank you very much for the information."

"You're welcome." The guard smiled at

them. "Now, enjoy the rest of your day at the museum. And please come see me if you think of any more questions."

"Okay." Michelle smiled. Then she pulled Cassie back toward the Australia exhibit, where Stephanie and the triplets were sitting on a bench. Michelle stopped a good distance away from them. She didn't want her sister to hear what she and Cassie were up to.

"Well?" Cassie asked. "What now?"

Michelle shrugged. "We stick to the plan," she said. "First we have to get over to the Rotunda. Once we're there, I bet we can figure out how to get backstage." She looked at the backpack on Cassie's shoulder. "Hey, can I have that back? I want to check on Al again before we get going."

Cassie handed over the backpack. "I'm sure he's fine," she said. "I made sure that nobody touched or kicked the bag while it was on the floor. It was right by my feet the whole time."

"Thanks." Michelle unzipped her bag the rest of the way. Then, she stuck her hand inside, and felt for Al's warm, fuzzy body.

But she couldn't find him. *Uh-oh,* she

thought. *Did he get cold and crawl under the towel?*

She pushed the towel aside. But she still couldn't find Al anywhere.

"What are you doing?" Cassie asked. She sounded a little impatient. "Come on, show me the bunny!"

"I can't!" Michelle blurted out. She yanked the towel out of her backpack, and pulled the bag open as wide as it would go. "Cassie!" she cried. "Al is *gone!*"

STEPHANIE

Chapter 9

Until today, Stephanie thought, *I had no idea what true embarrassment was. Now I could write a book on the subject.*

She still couldn't believe she'd gotten stuck on the exhibit like that. How totally humiliating. *The only thing to do right now is to forget about it and move on,* she told herself. *I still have a job to do. I have to be professional. Even if I don't feel so professional anymore.*

She took a deep breath. "Okay, guys," she said to the triplets. "I think maybe we've had enough of the animals. Why don't we try a different exhibit?"

"No!" Jimmy wailed. "More animals!"

Janie poked Stephanie in the side. "I'm hot," she said. "Can we go see the icebergs now?"

"I'm hungry," Jack announced.

"Hmm," Stephanie said. "Maybe the cafeteria isn't such a bad idea."

She definitely needed a break. Besides, how much trouble could the kids get into while they were eating?

"Hey, Michelle!" she called to her sister, who was huddled with Cassie near the door. "Heads up. We're going for a snack."

"YAAAAAY!" Jack cheered. Even Jimmy and Janie seemed to agree.

No one can argue with food, Stephanie thought. She checked a map of the museum on the wall nearby. *Ugh. Of course the cafeteria's all the way on the other end of the building. That figures.*

She looked at the triplets thoughtfully. How could she get all three of them safely across the museum?

I need something fun, she thought. *Something interesting.* She shot a glance at her sister. *Something that doesn't involve money.* She still felt a little annoyed about what Michelle had done. But she knew her sister was only trying to help.

"Okay, these are the snack-time rules," Stephanie announced. "We're going to have a parade!"

"A parade?" Jack looked suspicious. "I thought we were going to eat."

"We are," Stephanie assured him. "We're parading over to the cafeteria to get our snack. But the most important part of being in a parade is staying in line. So you have to march along right where I tell you to, okay?" The triplets nodded.

"Janie, you stay with Michelle. She'll hold your hand." Stephanie looked around for her sister.

Michelle was wandering around in a dark corner of the room with Cassie. *What's the matter with those two?* Stephanie thought. *They're worse than the triplets!* "Michelle? Earth to Michelle!"

Finally Michelle looked over. "What?"

Stephanie motioned to her impatiently. "Come on. I need you to hang on to Janie while we walk to the cafeteria."

Michelle looked unhappy about that for some reason. But Stephanie didn't have time to worry about why. She steered Janie in her sister's direction.

Then she grabbed the little boys' hands. "Okay, guys," she said. "You're with me. One, two, three, march!"

They stepped off, heading through the animal wing toward the front of the museum. "Left! Left! Left, right, left!" Stephanie called out. Jack and Jimmy strutted along like little soldiers beside Stephanie.

"Isn't that cute?" Stephanie heard someone say. She had to admit, the triplets were concentrating so hard on marching that it *was* really cute.

"Can I have anything I want for a snack?" Jack asked as they marched along.

"Sure," Stephanie agreed. She checked over her shoulder to make sure Michelle was following. "I guess so."

They entered the crowded museum cafeteria about five minutes later. "Okay, everybody," she said. "Find a seat. Then you can decide what you want to eat."

"Cookies!" Jack shrieked.

Stephanie winced. "Okay, okay." She guided Jack into a chair. "Cookies it is. What about you two?" She turned to Jimmy and Janie, who were already sitting down.

"I want French fries," Janie announced. "And I'm thirsty!"

"Me too!" Jimmy put in.

Jack stood up on his seat. "French fries!" he cried. Before Stephanie could stop him, he jumped down and began racing around the table.

"Jack, please sit!" Stephanie said firmly. She led him back to his place. "Now, you can have cookies *or* French fries. Not both."

Jack's face turned red. "But you said I can have any snacks I want!" he wailed.

Stephanie glanced around. *It's a good thing this place is so noisy,* she thought. Otherwise, Jack's voice would echo through the whole museum. "I said you could have any *snack* you wanted," she corrected. "*One* snack. Not two."

"Okay." Jack pouted. "Cookies."

"Great," Stephanie said. "Michelle, why

don't you and Cassie get our food? I'll stay here with the kids."

Michelle was sitting across the table, whispering with Cassie. She looked up and cleared her throat. "Um, actually, Steph, we'd like to take off," she said. "We're really not hungry. And we're, um, dying to see the Hall of Dinosaurs."

Janie's eyes widened. "Dinosaurs!" she cried. She popped out of her seat and ran around the table toward Michelle. "Take me, take me. I'm not hungry, either."

"Um, okay," Michelle said with a glance at Cassie. "I guess you can come with us if Steph says it's okay."

Stephanie grabbed her forehead. She felt like screaming. Why does Michelle keep doing this? she thought. *Every time I have things just about under control, she comes up with some other way to make everything crazy again!*

"Janie, please sit down," she said. "Nobody is going to the Hall of Dinosaurs right now. We'll go there later, I promise. But right now we're going to have a nice snack break."

Then Stephanie turned to face her sister. She

took a deep breath. "Look, Michelle," she said, trying to sound more patient than she felt. "I really wish you wouldn't keep trying to help here. Like I said earlier, I can handle this on my own. So please, *please,* just let *me* do the baby-sitting. Okay?"

Michelle frowned. "Fine," she said. "If you don't need any help, Cassie and I will just leave you alone and go over to the Hall of—"

"Not so fast." Stephanie wasn't about to let her sister wander off. What if Mrs. Havers came down from the office and saw her taking care of the triplets by herself?

"I don't need a second baby-sitter, but I could use a couple of waitresses." She grinned and handed over the snack money. "We need one box of cookies, and two servings of fries. No, make that three fries. I'm starving."

She sneaked a look at the triplets. They were giggling as they pulled napkins out of the napkin dispenser and turned them into hats. "Um, and three fruit juices and a soda. You can use any change that's left to get something for you and Cassie."

Michelle took the money with a sigh.

"Okay," she said. "Come on, Cassie. Let's hurry." The two of them took off in the direction of the cafeteria line.

Stephanie returned her attention to the triplets. They were just starting a very loud round of the snack song.

"Quiet!" Stephanie exclaimed. She clapped her hands over her ears to drown out the sound.

"Stephanie? Stephanie Tanner? Is that you?"

Stephanie dropped her hands from her ears. She looked up, startled. Standing in front of the table, holding a tray of sodas and French fries, was a petite woman with wavy black hair. She looked a bit familiar, Stephanie thought. "Um, hello," she said uncertainly.

The woman smiled. "I'm Beth Winters," she said. "From your aunt Becky's mommy group, remember? I booked your baby-sitting service for next weekend."

"Oh! Right!" Stephanie jumped to her feet. "Of course. Hi, Ms. Winters."

Yikes! she thought. *Ms. Winters really caught*

me at a bad moment. I've got to make sure I keep things together. If Ms. Winters thinks I can't handle the kids I'm baby-sitting today, she'll probably cancel her appointment—and tell all her friends to do the same thing.

She looked around the table quickly. Luckily, everything seemed to be more or less under control. For now, anyway.

"Actually, I'm glad I ran into you, Stephanie." Ms. Winters set her tray on the edge of the table and started digging around in her purse. "After I called you, I seem to have misplaced your phone number. I was going to get it from Becky at our next meeting, but as long as we're both here . . ." She pulled a pencil and notepad out of her purse and looked at Stephanie expectantly.

"Oh, okay. Sure." Stephanie was careful to keep smiling pleasantly. But out of the corner of her eye, she saw Jack leaning across the table. *What is he up to?* she wondered. "Um, my number is . . ."

She could only hope that she was reciting the correct phone number. Because as Ms. Winters carefully wrote down the information, Jack leaned over even farther—and grabbed a French fry off Ms. Winters's tray!

Don't turn around! Stephanie thought. *Please don't see Jack stealing your food!*

"Thank you so much, Stephanie," Ms. Winters said. She returned the pencil and notebook to her purse.

"You're welcome." While the woman was zipping up her purse, Stephanie nudged Jack back into his seat. *Gotcha,* she thought.

By the time Ms. Winters looked up, the only evidence of Jack's fry-jacking was a coating of salt on one of his cheeks.

Whew! That's one embarrassing situation avoided. Stephanie breathed a sigh of relief.

"Well, it was nice to see you," Ms. Winters said. "But I'd better get back to my family now."

"Yes," Stephanie said politely. "And I'd better get back to work."

Ms. Winters glanced at the triplets and smiled. "Oh!" she said. "Of course. I can see you have your hands full today. Well, good luck! And I'll see you next weekend."

"Great!" Stephanie kept smiling until Ms.

Winters was a safe distance away. Then she checked to see what the triplets were up to.

Jack jumped out of his seat. "Food!" he yelled, pointing.

Stephanie saw Michelle and Cassie heading toward them, each carrying a tray. "It's about time!" she muttered, relieved. Maybe now the kids would be distracted by their food for a while—and she could finally relax.

Michelle and Cassie set down the trays, and Stephanie passed out the food. For the next few minutes, she hardly had time to take a sip of her own soda or a bite of a French fry. She was too busy grabbing juice boxes to keep them from tipping over. Plus she had to keep stopping Jack from stuffing his mouth too full of cookies.

Stephanie was wiping a dribble of grape juice off Jack's face when she suddenly noticed that Janie was leaning forward in her chair. So far forward that her chin was nearly touching the table. "Hey," Stephanie said. "What are you doing?"

Janie sat back up and grinned, looking guilty. "Nothing."

"Really?" Stephanie said suspiciously. She

looked under the table. Just as she suspected. "Janie, why are your shoes off?"

The little girl shrugged. "My feet were hot."

Stephanie sighed and dove under the table. It took her only a minute or two to get Janie's shoes back on, but when she sat up, Jack wasn't in his seat.

"Hey!" she said to Jimmy. "Where's your brother?"

"He was still hungry," Jimmy explained.

Stephanie looked around nervously. "Jack!" she cried. She finally spotted him at a nearby table. He was just reaching for a little girl's piece of pie. "Stop! Don't touch that!"

She leaped to her feet and raced over, taking his hand just in time. Jack scowled. "I'm still hungry," he said.

"Sorry," Stephanie said to the little girl and her parents. "Excuse us, please."

She dragged Jack back to the table. Then she turned to check on Jimmy and Janie. Both of them were busy with their snacks.

Good. All present and accounted for, Stephanie thought with relief. *Man, watching triplets is way harder than I thought it would be.*

She sank back down into her own seat. *Wait a minute,* she thought suddenly. *Where's Michelle?*

Her younger sister was nowhere in sight. Neither was Cassie. Stephanie figured that the two of them must have gone back up to the line for more food.

Great, she thought. *Just because I told Michelle I didn't need her help all the time, that didn't mean she should go running off every two seconds. I could really use her right now. I feel like I'm totally going to lose it!*

She took a deep breath. *Stay professional,* she reminded herself. *Stay calm. Focus!*

Stephanie smiled at Jimmy. "So how's your grape juice?"

Jimmy took a small sip from his juice box and wrinkled his nose. "It doesn't taste like the grape juice Mommy makes us," he said.

"You know what, Jimmy?" Stephanie said. "That's because it's extra-special Imaginarium grape juice."

"I'll drink yours, Jimmy," Jack offered. He reached out and grabbed his brother's juice box.

Stephanie opened her mouth to protest. Just then, someone called her name. Ms. Winters and her family were waving to her on their way out.

"Bye!" Stephanie called cheerfully, waving back. "See you next weekend!"

Splash! Stephanie stopped dead. Something cold and wet was dripping down her face and splattering onto her arms. Startled, she glanced down at herself. The arms of her shirt were streaked with purple.

She spun around. Jack was holding the crushed grape juice box in his fist. "Oops," he said.

MICHELLE

Chapter 10

"I can't believe Al's gone," Michelle said. "I set my knapsack down for only a second!"

"I know," Cassie moaned. "But it was so dark in that Australia room. I guess the zipper was open just enough for him to hop out when we weren't looking. . . ."

Michelle and Cassie were walking down a hallway just outside the cafeteria. The hallway was crowded with people looking into the big display cases against the wall. The girls had no time to look at the pretty seashells or rocks inside. They had a bunny to find!

"This hall is pretty well lit," Cassie said. "There aren't any dark corners where a little bunny could hide."

"And we're kind of far from the place where Al disappeared," Michelle said. She stopped walking. "Let's think about this. Al's sick, right? So he probably couldn't get too far."

"Right," Cassie agreed. "But we have to find him before someone else does!"

Michelle nodded. "Let's go back to the Australia exhibit. That's where he got away, so that's where we should start looking."

"Okay," Cassie said as they started walking again. "But what about your sister? Isn't she going to be mad at us for leaving?"

Michelle shook her head. "No way. You heard her. She doesn't want my help. Besides we won't be gone long—and Al needs us! The sooner we find him—and Dr. Clause—the better off we'll be."

With the help of a map, she and Cassie quickly found their way back to the Australia room. It was a lot faster and easier getting through the museum without having to bring the triplets along. It didn't take the girls long to search every inch of the floor. Al was nowhere to be seen.

"What if he's hiding up on the platform somewhere?" Cassie asked worriedly.

Michelle looked at the desert scene. Her heart sank. It was full of rocks, animals, and plants. And most of them were bigger than a little bunny. *There are a zillion places in the exhibit where Al could be hiding,* Michelle thought.

Then she noticed something. "Hey, the light is a lot brighter up there," she pointed out to Cassie. "So Al probably wouldn't want to go that way. He's probably really scared being alone in a strange place like this. He'll want to go somewhere he feels safe. Someplace dark and quiet."

"I guess you're right," Cassie agreed.

"Let's try the next room then," Michelle suggested. "It's not too bright in there."

She and Cassie ran into the next room. This one had several displays showing the animals that lived in Antarctica. "Think like a bunny," Michelle instructed herself. "If you were a bunny where would you—"

"Look!" Cassie broke in. She pointed to one

of the exhibits. "Right there, in the middle of the penguins!"

Michelle peered over to where her friend was pointing. She gasped. There, tucked in between a couple of life-size penguins, was a fuzzy, brown-and-white creature.

"Al!" she cried.

Cassie looked around. "How are we going to get him out of there without anyone seeing us?" she whispered.

Michelle sized up the situation. A blond-haired guard was standing in the doorway, staring into the room. Aside from him, there were only a few people in the Antarctica room.

"I've got an idea," she said. She handed Cassie her backpack. "I'm going to cause a distraction. When the coast is clear, you hop up there and grab Al."

Cassie seemed nervous, but she nodded. "Okay. Uh, what kind of distraction?"

"You'll see." Michelle took a deep breath. She was nervous, too. But she knew what she had to do—for Al.

She quickly looked around. "Hey!" she cried. "There's Dr. Clause! The famous veterinarian from that TV show, *Paws and Clause.* Hurry. If we catch her maybe we can get her autograph."

"Dr. Clause?" a woman beside her said loudly. "Where?"

"She went that way." Michelle pointed to a long hallway outside the room.

Michelle heard the room fill up with excited murmurs. Soon, everyone piled out in search of Dr. Clause—including the security guard.

Now's our chance! Michelle thought. She glanced up at the exhibit again. The furry brown-and-white creature was still there.

"Well, what are we waiting for?" she cried to Cassie. She raced over to the display and hopped onto the platform. Cassie followed right behind her. "Here, Al," she called softly. "Here, little bun-bun . . ."

Her voice trailed off as she kneeled down and touched the brown-and-white fur. It felt strangely stiff. And then her fingers found a hard, plastic . . . beak?

"What is that?" she exclaimed in surprise.

Cassie leaned forward. "That's not Al at all!" she exclaimed. "It's a baby penguin."

"Oh, no!" Michelle heard voices outside the room. She and Cassie quickly jumped off the platform.

"That means we still don't know where he is!" Michelle exclaimed.

"Oh, Michelle!" Cassie wailed. "What if we never find him?"

"Don't say that. Don't even *think* it," Michelle commanded. "We will find him. We just have to keep looking. Now come on."

The girls set off through the museum again. They checked everywhere as they wandered through the rest of the animal wing. In one of the exhibits, they saw a few fake rabbits, but none of them looked anything like Al.

Finally Michelle and Cassie emerged in a stairwell across from the gift shop. "Should we look in there?" Cassie asked.

"Sure, I guess," Michelle said. "We have to look everywhere."

They entered the gift shop. There was a line of visitors at the front counter, waiting to buy postcards, T-shirts, or other museum souvenirs. Michelle and Cassie walked past the counter and started checking each aisle of the store.

"Boy, they sure do have a lot of stuff crammed in here," Cassie said. "There are lots of places Al could be hiding."

"Let's check it out." Michelle dropped to the floor. She crawled around on all fours. "Search every nook and cranny," she instructed. Cassie dropped to the floor beside her.

Michelle crawled up one aisle and down the other. No Al.

Then, in the corner of the store, she spotted a display of stuffed animals. The animals were placed in a crate that was turned on its side, so that it looked as if the animals were spilling out of the crate.

If I were Al, that would be a perfect place to hide, Michelle thought. *It's probably dark and soft and warm inside that pile of stuffed animals!*

"Cassie!" Michelle called. "I think I know where Al is!" She crawled over to the display. She began picking up the stuffed animals and flinging them into the aisle. "Al!" she cried. "Hold on! I'm coming to get you!"

When Michelle got to the bottom of the pile, all she found was an empty crate. No Al anywhere.

"Umm—excuse me. Miss?" a strange voice said.

Michelle gulped. She glanced up. A tall woman was standing over her. She wore a tag that said Manager.

"Did you want to *purchase* any of those stuffed animals?" the woman asked.

"Uh, no. I was just looking for . . . I mean, I just dropped my . . ."

"Come on, Michelle," Cassie interrupted. "I think I hear Stephanie calling us."

Cassie pulled her to her feet. "Sorry!" Michelle called. She and Cassie walked quickly out of the store.

Cassie stopped halfway down the hallway. "Okay. Where to next?"

Michelle thought for a second. "Maybe we should go straight to the Rotunda, just like we planned before," she said. "If we can find Dr. Clause, she might be able to tell us where to look for Al. After all, she *is* an animal expert."

Cassie's eyes lit up. "Good idea!"

"I think the Rotunda's this way," Michelle said, pointing.

Cassie pulled out her map and checked.

"You're right," she said. "Down this hall, through the lobby, around the corner just past the cafeteria, and up the west stairway. Then through the Hall of Dinos, and we're there."

"Let's go." Michelle took off. *We probably don't have much time before Dr. Clause will be too busy getting ready for her show to talk to us,* she thought as she and Cassie hurried down the hall. *Every minute counts!*

Finally the girls passed the wide, arched entrance to the cafeteria. The west stairway was just ahead.

Out of the corner of her eye, Michelle saw signs of a commotion inside the cafeteria. A group of people were gathered around one table—including several uniformed members of the cafeteria staff.

Hey, isn't that where we were sitting? Michelle thought.

She stopped short as she spotted her sister right in the middle of the crowd. Stephanie's hair was—wet. And her formerly white shirt was now purple. *Wow,* Michelle thought. *What happened?*

For a second she was tempted to go in to find out. What if Stephanie needed her help?

Then she remembered her sister's little speech that morning. *All you have to do is stay out of my way . . . I'm the baby-sitter here. . . .*

Michelle shrugged. Stephanie didn't want her help.

Besides, she thought, *I don't have much time left to find Al—not if I want Dr. Clause's help.*

She dodged past the doorway before Stephanie could spot her. Cassie was already a few yards ahead. "Come on, Michelle," she called. "We're almost there."

"Coming!" Michelle hurried after her.

Soon they were jogging through the Hall of Dinosaurs. Usually this was Michelle's favorite part of the Imaginarium. But today she hardly bothered to glance at the enormous skeletons and other fossils they were passing.

Cassie reached the auditorium first. "Here we are," she announced. "The Rotunda." She opened one of the doors and peeked inside. "Wow," she said. "It's dark in there."

"I guess Dr. Clause isn't here yet." Michelle felt let down for a moment. Then she brightened. "Hey! This is the perfect place for a scared bunny to hide. Dark, quiet . . ."

"Definitely!" Cassie agreed. "Come on, let's start looking."

Each of them took one side of the center aisle. *It's kind of spooky in here,* Michelle thought as she crawled between the rows of seats on her hands and knees. Just then she spotted something white under the seats in the next row over.

Her heart pounded with hope as she reached under the seat. "Here, Al," she crooned softly. "Don't be afraid, little bunny."

There was nothing there but a crumpled museum map.

Michelle sighed. She continued searching the row of seats. Then she turned down the next one. When she reached the end, Cassie was waiting for her.

"I don't think Al's in here," Cassie said sadly. "Maybe we should just—"

"Well! Hello, young ladies," a familiar woman's voice interrupted.

Michelle turned around, startled. Dr. Clause was standing right there behind them.

Cassie's jaw dropped. "You're—you're—" she stammered.

The vet smiled. "Let me guess," she said. "You girls thought you'd get here early so you could have front-row seats for my show."

"No," Michelle blurted out. " I mean, uh—not exactly—"

Tell her, Michelle thought. *Tell her about Al. Ask her where to look for him.* But she was so surprised to see the famous vet in person that her mouth didn't seem to be working right.

"I—uhh—" she stuttered.

"Hey, it's okay, I'm not going to yell at you." Dr. Clause chuckled. "I love all my fans. But I'm afraid you'll have to go outside and wait until the guards are ready to let people in here. Don't worry, the taping starts in less than an hour. So you won't have long to wait." She waved and started back down the aisle. "See you then, girls!"

Wait! Michelle wanted to cry, but it was too late. Dr. Clause hurried away and disappeared through a door in the side of the auditorium.

"Did you see that?" she exclaimed when she could finally speak again.

Cassie nodded. "Dr. Clause!" she said. She sounded totally shocked. "She looked just like she does on TV."

Now that she was starting to recover, Michelle grew angry with herself. *I missed the perfect chance to ask Dr. Clause about Al,* she thought. *Ugh, I messed up again.*

If I keep this up, Cassie may be right. I may never find Al. He may be lost forever!

STEPHANIE

Chapter 11

I can't believe this is happening, Stephanie thought. Grape juice was everywhere—all over the table, on the floor, on the chairs, and dripping down her face. *I've never been so humiliated in my life.*

People at other tables were pointing at her and laughing. Stephanie felt her face turn red with embarrassment.

She took a few deep breaths. *It was an accident,* she reminded herself. *Jack didn't mean to get grape juice on you. Or all over your favorite white shirt.*

She turned to the triplets. "Okay," she said through clenched teeth. "Come with me."

This time, all three kids came along immediately. *They must be afraid that I'm mad at them.* Stephanie felt bad at the thought.

"Don't worry, guys," she told them. She managed a small smile. "Everything's going to be okay. I just have to get cleaned up."

She looked around until she spotted a sign for restrooms at the back of the cafeteria.

"This way," she told the triplets.

When Stephanie reached the ladies' room, the boys stopped moving. They refused to go into the ladies' room. Only babies went in there with moms, they said. *Now* what was Stephanie supposed to do?

Well, one thing's for sure, Stephanie told herself. *I can't go on for one more minute with grape juice dripping down my neck. If I do, I'll lose it completely.*

Taking Janie by the hand, she gave Jimmy and Jack her most serious look.

"Okay," she said. "I'll agree, but this is what we're going to do. Janie and I are going into the bathroom. You two are going to stay right here. Right outside the door, right next to each other, until we come out. And don't talk to anyone. Got it?"

The two boys nodded. Stephanie pointed to the cafeteria line, which Jack and Jimmy could see across the room. "Michelle and her friend will be coming through that line any second. When you see them, run over there and tell them where I am. Ask them to stay right here with you until I come out. Can you do that?"

"Yes. I think so," Jimmy said. Jack nodded beside him.

"Good. Come on, Janie." Stephanie pushed through the door into the bathroom with the little girl in tow.

There was nobody else in the long, narrow room, so she let go of Janie's hand. "Stay right here," she warned her.

Then she checked out the damage in the row of mirrors over the sinks. It was even worse than she'd thought. Grape juice was dripping down her face, and her hair was plastered to her cheeks in a sticky mess.

"Ugh!" she said to her reflection. "Why didn't I make them drink water?"

She sighed and got to work. First she scrubbed the grape juice off her face and neck. Then she rubbed herself dry with paper towels. Next she leaned over one of the sinks and did her best to rinse out her hair under the tap. By the time she was pretty sure that most of the purple mess was gone, her hair was soaked. So was most of her blouse. Luckily, she had a sweater tied around her waist. She took it off and pulled it over her head.

"There," Stephanie told her reflection. "Not great, but definitely better."

Stephanie stopped short. Wait a minute. Janie was being awfully quiet. She glanced over her shoulder. "Janie?" she called. "Where are you?"

The little girl appeared at the end of the row of toilet stalls. "I'm right here," she said.

"Good." Stephanie smiled with relief. Then she returned her attention to her hair. She tried to wring it out, but it was still sopping wet. Then she noticed the hot-air hand dryer on the wall. "Aha!" she said. "It's great that public restrooms have paper towels *and* these things."

She turned on the dryer and stuck her head in front of it. After hitting the On button three or four times, her hair was dry enough. She lifted her sweater and turned the dryer on once more to dry off her shirt a bit. Finally she was ready to go.

"Okay, Janie!" she called. "Let's go."

The little girl immediately appeared around the corner of the stalls again. "I'm ready," she said brightly.

"Terrific." Stephanie reached to take the little girl's hand. Then she did a double take. "Hold it," she said. "What happened to your shoes?"

Janie shrugged. "My feet were hot."

Stephanie groaned. *Think,* she instructed herself. *When was the last time you looked at Janie's feet?*

"Where did you take off your shoes, Janie? Was it in here, or . . ." She was afraid to imagine where else Janie might have left them. Under the table in the cafeteria? Hidden in the Australia exhibit? Back in her parents' car? *No,* Stephanie realized, *I definitely remember putting Janie's shoes back on in the cafeteria.* They had to be somewhere nearby.

Janie bit her lip and glanced over her shoulder. "Um . . . I hid them," she said. "I don't want to wear them anymore."

"Okay," Stephanie said, in a gentle, friendly voice. "Now tell me *where* you hid them."

Janie pointed at one of the stalls. Stephanie hurried into it and looked around. The shoes weren't on the floor, or on top of the toilet paper dispenser. They weren't on the back of the tank.

"I give up, Janie," Stephanie said. "Now tell me where they really—" She cut herself off with a gasp. "Oh, *no!*"

Janie giggled. "I told you I hid them," she said proudly.

Stephanie leaned forward. "You hid them—in the *toilet?"*

"All wet!" Janie said happily. "Now I can't wear them."

"Want to bet?" Stephanie muttered.

She knew she needed to get the shoes out of the toilet before someone came in and saw them—or flushed them! But first, she hurried to the door and poked her head out.

To her relief, Jimmy and Jack were still standing right outside. "How's it going, guys?" she asked.

"Michelle didn't come out yet," Jimmy reported.

"That's okay," Stephanie said. "Just stay put. And keep watching for Michelle. We'll be out soon."

She ducked back inside the bathroom and headed for the stall. Stepping inside, she gazed into the toilet. Sure enough, the small canvas shoes were floating gently in the blue-tinted water. Janie stood just outside the stall, watching.

Stephanie looked around helplessly. How was she going to get the shoes out of the toilet bowl? Finally she realized there was only one way. She wrinkled her nose. "Here I go," she said. In one quick motion, she reached in the toilet and grabbed them.

"Out of my way!" she cried. She raced out of the stall with the shoes.

She tossed the shoes into the nearest sink. Then she turned the hot water on full blast and stuck her hands underneath. She used about half the soap in the dispenser scrubbing her hands. Then she used the rest of the soap on Janie's shoes. She scrubbed them, then rinsed them over and over. By the time she was satisfied that they were clean enough, the sink was full of soap suds. The mirrors were coated in steam.

Finally she picked up the shoes and shook off some of the excess water. "There," she said. "All clean. Let's put them on."

"Can't," Janie insisted. "Wet!"

"Not for long." Stephanie carried the shoes over to the hand dryer. Hitting the button, she toasted them for a couple of rounds until they were only slightly damp. "There you go. Nice and dry. Now let's put them on and get out of here."

A couple of elderly women came into the ladies' room while Stephanie was wrestling with Janie's feet. They raised their eyebrows and clucked at the steamy, soapy, water-splattered bathroom. Stephanie didn't pay any attention. Jimmy and Jack had been outside by themselves for an awfully long time. She wanted to get back to them right away.

I just hope Michelle found them, she thought. *She must be through the line by now.*

"Okay, Janie," she said when the shoes were safely back on the little girl's feet. "That's better. Now come on, let's get back to your brothers."

She took Janie's hand and headed through the door.

"Okay, boys," she sang out. "All set. Let's—"

She cut herself off when she saw that Jack was standing there—alone. As in, without his brother.

"I'm hungry," the little boy said when he spotted her.

"Umm—where's Jimmy?" Stephanie asked. Suddenly her throat felt kind of tight. "And Michelle—where's Michelle?"

Jack shrugged. "I don't know," he said.

Stephanie felt panic rush over her. *Stay calm,* she told herself. *A good baby-sitter does* not *lose her cool in an emergency.*

She glanced around wildly, but there was no sign of the little boy.

No, she thought. *This can't be.*

I lost Jimmy!

MICHELLE

Chapter 12

Michelle checked her watch and gulped. "Fifteen minutes left until Dr. Clause's show," she told Cassie.

Cassie bit her lip. "What if we don't find Al before the taping starts? What if we never take him to see Dr. Clause?"

Michelle didn't think about that. She couldn't. "We have to find him. We just have to," she said grimly. "Come on, let's keep looking."

"But we've already looked through the whole museum," Cassie wailed.

"We didn't really search the cafeteria,"

Michelle pointed out. "Or the third floor. . . ." She let her voice trail off. *How are we supposed to find one small bunny in such a big place?* she wondered.

Right now, they were back in the animal wing, not far from the site of Al's escape.

Suddenly Michelle noticed a red-haired security guard standing in the doorway. "Hey!" she said, grabbing Cassie by the arm. "Check it out. Isn't that the guard that was so nice to us before?"

Cassie looked. "It's him, all right."

"Well, maybe he can help us find Al. He must know every inch of this museum. So maybe he knows some good hiding places where we could look."

Cassie looked doubtful. "But what if he gets mad at us for bringing a rabbit into the museum? We could be in big trouble."

Michelle shrugged. She wasn't going to think about that now. All she cared about was finding Al. She was running out of time—and she was desperate.

She hurried up to the guard. "Hi," she said. "Remember us?"

The guard smiled. "Why sure!" he said. "Where's your sister stuck this time?"

Michelle laughed weakly. "It's nothing like that," she told him. "Actually, it's more like *my* problem. See, I kind of brought my class's pet rabbit to the museum today to see Dr. Clause. But he got out of my bag and ran away. Now we can't find him."

"Right," Cassie agreed. "See, he was looking kind of sick. We thought if anyone could help him, Dr. Clause could."

The guard looked startled. "You mean your pet rabbit got away from you here in the *museum?"*

"Yes." Michelle gazed at him hopefully. "So can you help us find him?"

The guard shook his head sadly. "I'm sorry, but I'm on duty, miss," he said, his voice kind. "I can't leave this area. I'm afraid I can't help you."

Michelle couldn't believe her ears. "But you have to help us," she begged. "Please! We have to find Al."

"I'm sorry," the guard said. "All I can do is keep an eye out for him. I promise I'll let you know if I spot him. But from now on, remember this," he added. "A museum isn't really a good place to bring a pet."

"I know," Michelle said quietly. "Well, thanks anyway. Come on, Cassie. We'd better go search some more."

She ran away, not wanting the guard to see the tears filling her eyes.

We have to find Al, Michelle thought. *There's no way he could be missing for good. If he was, what would she tell everyone at school tomorrow?*

"Hey, Michelle, wait up!" Cassie said, hurrying behind her.

Michelle slowed down. She blinked back her tears. "Well? Where should we look next?" she asked her friend.

Cassie glanced around uncertainly. They were standing in a room about birds. Eggs of all shapes and sizes filled the display cases. "I don't know," she said. "But pretty soon we'll have to—"

"Uh-oh!" Michelle interrupted. A woman was coming toward them with a big smile on her face. She was holding a little girl by the hand. "Isn't that the lady Steph was talking to before?" Michelle asked.

"I think so," Cassie whispered as the woman reached them.

"Well, hello!" the woman said. "Are you all enjoying your day?"

"Um, sure, uh . . ." Frantically, Michelle searched her mind for the woman's name.

The woman smiled broadly. "It's Ms. Winters," she said. "And this is my daughter, Caitlin. Where are the others in your group?"

"Others?" Michelle said blankly. Suddenly she remembered that she was supposed to be helping Stephanie baby-sit. Or at least she was supposed to *look* like she was helping. "Er, they're, um, back that way." She chose a random direction and pointed.

Ms. Winters seemed confused. "Really? I just came from there," she said. "I didn't see your sister or the triplets."

Michelle gulped. Maybe Stephanie was acting a little bossy today, but Michelle didn't want to mess up her baby-sitting business. And if Ms. Winters thought Michelle was goofing off with her friend instead of helping, it would make both of them look really bad.

"Did I say that way?" she corrected herself. "I

meant, uh—" She suddenly broke off. A little boy wandered toward them, pausing to look at the cases of eggs. *A very familiar-looking little boy.*

"There!" Michelle blurted, pointing. "See? There's Jimmy now!"

Cassie's jaw fell open in surprise. Michelle nudged her, and Cassie's jaw snapped shut before Ms. Winters could see.

Michelle hurried over and grabbed Jimmy's hand. "Don't wander off, now," she told him. She tried to sound mature and responsible, like a good baby-sitting assistant.

Jimmy looked up at her and smiled. "Okay, Michelle!" he said.

Ms. Winters smiled. Michelle thought she looked a little relieved. She glanced at her watch. "Well, girls, you'll have to excuse us. We came today to see the taping of *Paws and Clause,* and it's going to be starting soon. It's Caitlin's favorite TV show."

"Okay," Michelle said. "Have fun." She shot Cassie a worried glance. Ms. Winters and her daughter rushed off.

The taping was starting in just a few minutes. They were almost out of time!

Michelle looked down at Jimmy. The little boy was staring at an ostrich egg.

"Hey, Jimmy," Michelle said. "Where's Stephanie?"

Jimmy shrugged. "Don't know," he said. "I guess she got lost when I went to chase the bunny."

Michelle's heart stopped. "Wait! What did you say?"

"She's lost," Jimmy repeated patiently.

"No, no!" Cassie cried. "The part about the bunny! Did you see a bunny?"

"Uh-huh!" Jimmy turned away from the egg. "I was standing by the bathroom with Jack. We had to wait a long time. A *really* long time. And then I saw the bunny. So I followed it. But then I didn't know where Steph'nie was anymore."

Yes! Michelle's heart gave a little leap. *Jimmy has seen Al! Jimmy can help me find Al!*

She kneeled down in front of the little boy and took him by both shoulders. "Jimmy, tell me exactly what the bunny looked like," she said. "And then tell me where you saw it last."

"It was a brown-and-white bunny," Jimmy said. "He was running around in the food place. I think he was eating stuff off the floor. Then he ran away, so I followed him."

"You followed him back here?" Michelle asked.

Jimmy shrugged. "Nope. I came here to see more animals. And I wanted to find Steph'nie, too. I don't like her being lost." He looked sad.

"Don't worry, Jimmy," Michelle reassured him. "Cassie and I will help you find Stephanie and the others soon, I promise."

"Okay." Jimmy looked relieved.

"But do you know what? That bunny you saw is lost, too." Cassie put in.

"That's right," Michelle went on. "And we need you to help us find him, Jimmy. Do you think you can do that?"

"Yeah! I'd like to do that." The little boy nodded.

"Good." Michelle exchanged a glance with Cassie. "Now, think very hard," she told the little boy. "Try to remember where the bunny was when you saw it last."

"The bunny was, um . . ." Jimmy frowned.

"That way," he said finally, pointing back toward the animal wing. "I think."

"Great, Jimmy," Michelle said. "Let's go." *It's worth a try,* she told herself. *He's only four years old. But he's our best chance at finding Al!*

STEPHANIE

Chapter 13

This is a nightmare! Stephanie felt her whole body tremble. *I can't believe I actually lost a kid! What am I going to do?*

She knew she had to get a grip if she wanted to find Jimmy. She took a moment to calm herself—even if it was only a little bit. "Okay, Jack," she said in a no-nonsense tone. "You must have seen Jimmy leave, right? So which way did he go?"

"I'm hungry," Jack said, sounding grouchy.

"You're always hungry," Janie accused him.

Jack stuck out his tongue at her. "Am not!"

"Are, too!"

"Kids, hey!" Stephanie put a hand on her forehead. Everything was suddenly spinning out of control. "Quiet! Come on, now. We have to figure out where your brother went. It is *very* important. Now, Jack, did your brother go over there, toward the food line? Or into the men's bathroom, maybe? Or where?"

Jack shrugged. "Don't know," he muttered. "That way?" He pointed toward the main cafeteria doors.

Stephanie gulped. *That's what I was afraid of,* she thought. *Jimmy went into the main museum. That means he could be anywhere.*

"Okay," she said, trying to sound calm. "Then let's go that way and look for him. Come on."

Stephanie grabbed both kids by their hands and headed for the doors. She tried not to imagine all the horrible things that could happen to Jimmy while he wandered around the museum all alone. Then another thought occurred to her. What if he wandered *out* of the museum?

I've got to find him—and fast! Stephanie thought. *He could be in danger. And it's all my fault!*

For the first time in a while, Stephanie thought about Michelle. Where on earth were her sister and Cassie? She wished she hadn't been so quick to tell them she didn't need their help. She sure could use it now.

What should she do first, she wondered. Talk to a guard? Maybe have Jimmy paged over the museum's intercom?

No, not yet, Stephanie decided. *Mrs. Havers is right upstairs and Jimmy probably didn't get very far. I'll look for him myself first. I don't want to worry Mrs. Havers if Jimmy is perfectly fine.*

She looked up the hallway in one direction, then down the other. Which way would a little boy go?

"Steph'nie!" Janie complained. "My feet *are wet!* I *have* to take off my shoes *now!*"

"No, Janie!" Stephanie snapped. "I said you have to leave them on. So stop asking, okay?"

Janie looked hurt, and Stephanie bit her lip. It was getting so hard to hold on to both of the kids and think about where to find Jimmy at the same time.

She wished there was someone around to help her out. For the first time, Stephanie wished her sister was her baby-sitting partner for real.

Maybe if I'd let Michelle help more, she would be here right now, she thought. *I guess I was kind of extreme about not wanting her help. And look where that got me. . . .*

"All right, let's try this way," she said finally. She pointed down the aisle. "Maybe Jimmy went back to the animal wing. He really liked it there."

As they reached the big *Animals, Animals, Animals* sign, Stephanie glanced at a map on the wall under the sign and gulped. The animal wing was pretty big. She and the triplets had seen only part of it before.

Maybe I should find that nice guard who rescued me earlier, Stephanie thought. *He might have seen Jimmy if he came through this way. And I'm sure he would have remembered him from the little incident on the exhibit.*

Still holding tightly to Janie's and Jack's hands, Stephanie checked quickly through the first few rooms. In the Africa exhibit, Stephanie spotted a little boy with brown hair standing in front of a poster of a lion.

"Jimmy!" she cried, flooded with relief. She raced forward with Jack and Janie. She dropped their hands to give the little boy a big hug. "Thank goodness!" she exclaimed. "I was afraid you were—"

She stopped as the little boy looked up at her in surprise. He wasn't Jimmy! He was a total stranger.

Stephanie gulped. "Oops!" She quickly let go of the boy. "Sorry about that, little buddy. I thought you were someone else."

The boy just blinked at her, looking confused. Stephanie slumped against the wall. Where was Jimmy?

Stephanie glanced down at the other two triplets. Janie was sitting on the floor, yanking at her left shoe. Jack was looking at a display about the food chain.

"Oh, no, you don't!" Stephanie called, hurrying toward the little girl. "Leave that on!" She helped Janie to her feet and took Jack's hand. "Come on," she said. "We have to keep looking for Jimmy."

Jack was staring hungrily into a glass case displaying all different kinds of human food, from doughnuts to fried chicken. "Look," he told Stephanie. "Snacks!"

"They're plastic," Stephanie told him.

Jack frowned. "No, they're not," he insisted.

Okay, whatever, Stephanie thought. She didn't have time to argue. The longer they stood here, the farther away Jimmy might be getting.

She and the two remaining triplets continued on through the animal wing. Jimmy was nowhere to be found. Finally they emerged into a quiet, empty area between wings. The only thing there was a wide marble staircase. A sign pointed up the stairs to the Hall of Dinosaurs and the Rotunda auditorium.

Exhausted, Stephanie sank down on the bottom step to think about what to do next. Janie and Jack plunked down next to her.

This is terrible, Stephanie thought. Tears pricked her eyes. *Jimmy could be in real trouble. And it's my fault!*

She took a deep breath and sat up straighter. She knew what she had to do now. *This has gone far enough. I have to get some help. Starting with having Jimmy paged and alerting all the guards to search for him.*

She sighed. When word of this disaster got out, Mrs. Havers would be worried sick. And it would probably mean the end of her baby-sitting business. That didn't seem very important at the moment. The only thing that mattered was finding Jimmy and making sure he was safe.

Suddenly Stephanie spied a movement out of the corner of her eye. She jumped up from the stairs, startled. Then she saw a flash of brown fur in the dark space between the stairs and the wall.

"Yikes," she said aloud. "A rat!"

She glanced at Jack and Janie. They were a safe distance away from the yucky creature. Jack was helping Janie unbuckle one of her shoes. They weren't paying any attention to Stephanie at all.

Ugh, she thought, looking back at the rat's hiding place. She backed away a few steps. *I guess I should tell someone about this when I talk to the guards. What if it bites someone?*

Just then the creature moved again. It was moving toward a patch of sunlight. Stephanie was about to grab the kids and run when she spotted a pair of long brown ears and a pink nose emerging into the light.

"Whew!" Stephanie chuckled with relief. "It's not a rat at all. It's just a bunny."

What was a rabbit doing hopping around loose in the museum? As far as she knew, the Imaginarium didn't have a petting zoo.

Then she remembered the signs in the lobby about that animal show. *That's it,* she thought. *He must have escaped from the taping somehow.*

As she leaned forward for a closer look, the rabbit hopped all the way out from its hiding place.

Stephanie did a double take as she got a better look at the little creature. "Wait a minute," she muttered. "That's no TV bunny! That's Michelle's class rabbit, smelly old Al! What in the world is *he* doing here?"

There wasn't time to think about that now. She scooped up the bunny and called to Jack and Janie. It was time to face the music—and get some serious help finding Jimmy.

MICHELLE

Chapter 14

"Are you *sure* this was where you saw him?" Michelle looked around the Hall of Dinosaurs uncertainly. It was crowded with people, including a long line of visitors inching their way forward into the Rotunda for the *Paws and Clause* taping.

"I think so." Jimmy blinked. "I remember there were some big bones around. 'Cause the bunny hopped behind one when he saw me."

Michelle chewed on her lip. *There are bones all over the museum,* she thought. *Not just in the dinosaur exhibit.*

"Hey!" Jimmy cried, sounding excited. He

pointed toward a door nearby. "That door was open before! Maybe the bunny went in there!"

Michelle looked at the door. It was painted green and tucked into the wall between two glass cases full of fossils. There was no sign on it saying Keep Out or anything.

"Come on," she told Cassie and Jimmy. "Let's see if we can get in there. Al might be trapped inside!"

She hurried over and tried the knob. It turned easily. When the door swung open, Michelle saw a long, narrow room filled with people. They were scurrying around busily, carrying clipboards and stacks of papers. There were pieces of large equipment standing around, too: huge spotlights, a microphone on a tall stand, and other items that Michelle didn't recognize.

"What *is* this place?" Cassie wondered.

Michelle didn't know. And she didn't really care. All she cared about was finding Al. "Come on," she said. "Let's start searching."

She checked to make sure that Cassie was holding Jimmy's hand. Then she turned to peek under some shelves that lined one wall.

"Ouch!" Michelle cried as someone bumped into her. She stood up and saw a young man hurrying past. He barely glanced at her.

"Sorry," he called over his shoulder, sounding distracted.

Michelle frowned and rubbed her hip. Then she went back to her search.

I hope Al's not too scared in here, she thought worriedly. *All this rushing around and yelling must be making him pretty nervous. I bet he's definitely hiding under some of these shelves. Or maybe he's in a dark corner somewhere.*

Michelle got down on her hands and knees. "Come on," she told Cassie and Jimmy. "We need to stay low if we want to see Al."

The two of them crouched down beside her. Then they all started peering under the shelves, the equipment, and anything else they passed. They continued to crawl through the room on their hands and knees, checking every inch of the way.

Michelle heard heavy footsteps behind her.

She quickly sat up, afraid someone else would run into her. A man with a beard looked down at her and frowned.

"Hey," he said. "You kids are late! We're already starting!"

"What?" Michelle asked, startled. "Um, I think you must be mistaking us for someone else."

It was too late. The man was already rushing off, calling to a dark-haired woman nearby. She hurried over and bustled Michelle, Cassie, and Jimmy into another room before they could protest. "Just wait in here," she told them briskly. "Someone will be with you when it's time."

"Time for what?" Cassie murmured as the woman closed the door behind her.

Michelle shrugged. "I have no idea. But we might as well check around for Al in here, too." The room was small and very dimly lit. At one end a heavy-looking velvet curtain was hanging from floor to ceiling. "Actually, this is just the kind of dark, cozy place Al might want to hide. Make sure you check all the corners."

"Okay," Cassie said. "I just hope we can see him if he's in here. Why don't they turn on some lights? I can hardly see my hand in front of my face."

"Just feel your way around," Michelle suggested. She crawled ahead toward the curtain. "He knows us, so he probably won't hop away if he smells us coming. All we have to do is find him."

She kept her face close to the floor as she crawled along, hoping to spot the flash of the little bunny's shiny eyes or his brown-and-white fur.

Suddenly there was a flash of light. It was so bright that Michelle was momentarily blinded. "What—" she exclaimed. She slapped her hands over her eyes.

She couldn't see, but she could hear the sound of people clapping. *What is going on here?* Michelle wondered.

"Well, hello!" a familiar voice said.

Michelle peeked through her fingers. *Uh-oh,* she thought. *I think I know what's going on here. And it's not good.*

"Welcome, kids," the voice said. "Please come on out here, and bring your little friend with you."

Michelle blinked hard a few times, trying to get used to the bright light. She saw that the curtain had opened, revealing a large, well-lit area. Several chairs and a large table were set up nearby. A person was sitting in one of the chairs.

"Dr. Clause!" Jimmy yelled, hurrying forward. "You're my favorite show!"

There was a rumble of laughter from the audience.

"Yikes." Michelle whispered to Cassie. "I think we just accidentally walked—uh, crawled—into the middle of the *Paws and Clause* taping!"

Dr. Clause smiled and waved for Michelle and Cassie to join her. Jimmy had already hopped up onto one of the empty chairs. He grinned broadly at the doctor.

Michelle felt her face turn bright red. She got to her feet and walked slowly in the vet's direction. *This is the most humiliating moment of my life!* she thought.

"Don't be shy, kids," Dr. Clause said as Michelle and Cassie came up. "Sit down here by me and—"

The vet paused. "But wait. Where's your pet?"

"Pet?" Michelle repeated. "Uh—"

The vet glanced from one of the kids to the other. "Yes, your pet. Where is it?"

Michelle shot Cassie a panicky glance. How were they going to get out of this? "Um . . ."

"Wait!" a new voice called from the side of the stage. "Here's their pet!"

STEPHANIE

Chapter 15

Stephanie raced onto the stage, ignoring the thin young man who tried to stop her. "Here's their pet!" she shouted again. She held Al up with both hands. "It's a bunny rabbit."

"Al!" Michelle cried out. "There you are. Thank goodness."

"Ah," Dr. Clause reached up and took the bunny from Stephanie. "My, my! Such a cute little thing he is, too!"

Stephanie collapsed against one of the chairs, winded from her race for the Rotunda. *Whew!* she thought. *It's a good thing I happened to look up at that monitor—just in time to see the curtain going up on Michelle, Cassie, and Jimmy!*

She grinned at her sister. Michelle was staring at Al in shock. *And it's a pretty good thing Al and I happened to be right down the hall too—just close enough for a dramatic entrance.*

Jack and Janie ran up to their brother. All three triplets tried to squash themselves into the same chair. The audience chuckled.

Suddenly Stephanie remembered where she was. On a TV show! Her face flamed with embarrassment.

"Oops," she said with a weak grin. "Uh, sorry to interrupt."

"That's quite all right," Dr. Clause said kindly. She held up Al so the audience could see him. "Now, let's take a good look at this little fellow here. . . ."

The next few minutes passed in a blur. Stephanie stood behind the vet while Dr. Clause examined Al the bunny. Dr. Clause talked all the while about caring for pet rabbits.

Finally she handed the bunny back to Michelle. "I have good news," she told her. "Little Al is just fine. Fit as a fiddle."

"Really?" Michelle said. "But he accidentally ate some candy yesterday. He seemed kind of sick. . . ."

The vet nodded. "He probably had a tummy ache." She reached over and patted Al gently on the head. "You should always be careful about what you feed any of your pets. Some things that are perfectly harmless to people can be bad for some animals. For instance, chocolate is very dangerous to dogs."

"Really?" Jimmy piped up. "I want a dog. Mommy and Daddy say I have to wait till I'm older."

The crowd laughed. Dr. Clause smiled. "Your mommy and daddy know what's best," she said. She turned back to Michelle again. "But it seems that whatever Al ate only disagreed with him a little bit. You should keep an eye on him for a couple of days, just to make sure. And you can take him to your own vet if he starts to look sick again. But for now, I would say he's in perfect health."

"Oh, thank you!" Michelle looked overjoyed. "I've been worrying about him all day."

So that's why Al is here. And that's why Michelle kept disappearing, Stephanie thought. *Michelle brought Al to see Dr. Clause!*

Soon the vet's assistant was ushering them all off the stage. Dr. Clause announced her next guest. The six of them—plus Al—stood in the hallway outside the side door of the stage.

Stephanie immediately grabbed Jimmy and hugged him. "Boy, am I glad to see *you!*" she told him. "You gave me a real scare."

Jimmy wrinkled his nose at her. "Why?" he asked. "*You're* the one who was lost."

Cassie was still staring at the stage door behind them. "Boy," she said. "That sure was weird!"

"I know." Michelle said. She cuddled Al in her arms. "I can't believe we accidentally ended up on stage in the middle of the show! But at least Al is—"

She stopped short and stared at Stephanie. "Hey, wait a minute! How did you find Al, anyway? And how did you find *us?*"

Stephanie quickly explained about finding Al on the staircase—and about seeing them on the monitor. "I was on my way to the museum office to make an announcement," she said. "At first I was so relieved to see Jimmy that I didn't even notice where you all were. Then I saw Dr. Clause. I figured you could probably use a little visit from good old Al right about then."

"You got that right," Michelle told her sister. "Whew!"

"How did *you* find Al?" Cassie asked. "We were searching for him everywhere."

"Yeah!" Michelle agreed. "I mean, you didn't even know he was here. You didn't know he was lost, either."

Stephanie grinned. "I just followed the yucky smell, and there he was," she joked. She patted Al apologetically. "Just kidding, pal. Actually he sort of found *me*."

Michelle bit her lip. "I'm sorry about bringing him," she said softly. "I really messed up." She unzipped her backpack and tucked Al inside. "I guess I should have told you."

Stephanie shrugged. "Don't worry about it. After everything else that happened today, a stowaway bunny doesn't seem like that big of a deal." She paused. "Listen, Michelle, I just want to say that I'm sorry, too."

"Sorry for what?" Michelle asked.

"Well, I was acting kind of bossy before," Stephanie said. "I thought I didn't need your help. But I guess I did. It took me awhile to realize it, but the Haverses were right to insist on two baby-sitters. The triplets are just too much for me to handle on my own."

She smiled. "Maybe some of your baby-sitting ideas weren't so hot, but I should have at least explained why. Then maybe you could have helped out for real." She paused. "Maybe then Jimmy wouldn't have gotten lost."

"Um, thanks, Steph. But I guess it was my fault, too," Michelle admitted. "I shouldn't have gone off and left you alone."

Stephanie nodded. "That's okay. All's well that ends well, right?"

"Right," Michelle and Cassie said at the same time.

Stephanie checked her watch. "Oops!" she said. "I sort of lost track of the time. Come on, we'd better get back to the lobby. Mrs. Havers should be there any minute now."

She grabbed Jack's hand. Michelle grabbed Janie's. Cassie took Jimmy's. Then they all headed down the hall toward the nearest staircase.

Both Mr. and Mrs. Havers were waiting by the horse statue in the lobby when they arrived. "Mommy!" Janie cried, racing over. "Daddy!" The boys whooped and followed their sister. Stephanie felt happy and relieved as she watched the family hug. Then she stepped forward.

"Hi," she said. "Here we are."

Mrs. Havers smiled at her. "Did you have a nice day?" she asked. "Any problems?"

Stephanie hesitated. *Where do I start?* she wondered. She knew she had to tell the Havers about everything that had happened.

"No problems at all," Michelle spoke up before Stephanie could answer. "Especially since my friend Cassie came along to help us. We had one baby-sitter for each triplet!"

"It was fun!" Jimmy spoke up. "We saw lots of animals!"

Janie nodded. "Steph'nie's the best baby-sitter we ever had," she said. "Even though she made me wear these itchy old shoes the whole time."

Mr. and Mrs. Havers laughed. "Wonderful!" Mr. Havers said. "Well, then. Should we get on home?"

"Yes!" Jack cried. "I'm hungry!"

Everyone laughed. Stephanie shot Michelle a grateful look as they all trooped out of the museum toward the minivan at the curb. She knew she still had to tell the triplets' parents the truth. But it could wait until a little later, when she could speak to them in private.

Whew, Stephanie thought. For the first time, she realized how tired she was. *I'm so glad this baby-sitting job is over. Parts of it were fun, just like I expected. But there were a few parts I could have lived without.*

As they reached the van, Mr. Havers suddenly stopped and looked at Stephanie. "Oh!" he said. "I just remembered. My wife and I are going to a party next Thursday night. Would you and Michelle be available to baby-sit then?"

Michelle glanced at her, obviously trying

not to laugh. Stephanie bit her lip to stop herself from grinning.

Thursday?

Stephanie still thought the kids were adorable. But she needed a little more time to recover before she could even *think* about baby-sitting the Haverses' triplets again.

"Gosh, I'm so sorry!" she told the Havers quickly. "I wish we could, but we happen to be busy that night."

She smiled. "I'll check with my business partners, Darcy and Allie, though. I'm sure they'd just *love* to baby-sit for you!"

Minstrel ® Books

Sweepstakes

Sponsors Official Rules:

No Purchase Necessary.

Enter by mailing this completed Official Entry Form (no copies allowed) or by mailing a 3" x 5" card with your name and address, daytime telephone number and birthdate to the Pocket Books/ "Full House Sisters Sweepstakes", 1230 Avenue of the Americas, 13th Floor, NY, NY 10020. Entry forms are available in the back of Full House Sisters #6: Will You Be My Valentine? (2/00), #7: Let's Put On a Show (3/00) and #8: Baby-sitters, Incorporated (4/00), on in-store book displays and on the web site SimonSays.com. Sweepstakes begins 2/1/00. Entries must be postmarked by 4/30/00 and received by 5/15/00. Not responsible for lost, late, damaged, postage-due, stolen, illegible, mutilated, incomplete, or misdirected or not delivered entries or mail or for typographical errors in the entry form or rules or for telecommunications system or computer software or hardware errors or data loss. Entries are void if they are in whole or in part illegible, incomplete or damaged. Enter as often as you wish, but each entry must be mailed separately. Winners will be selected at random from all eligible entries received in a drawing to be held on or about 5/25/00. Winners will be notified by mail. The grand prize winner will be notified by phone as well. Odds of winning depend on number of eligible entries received.

Prizes: One Grand Prize: Two backpacks full of identical arts and crafts items (for winner and a friend). Items include: 2 backpacks, 2 "Passport to Paris" videos from Warner Home Video, 2 Girl's Best Friend Club (secret message recorders), 2 Body Art Activity Cases, 2 Friendship Fun packs, 2 Mini-stamper Sets, 2 Fun Pencil Bags, 2 Sketchbooks, 2 buckets of sidewalk chalk, 2 Scenstationary packs, 2 True Girlz accessory packs, 2 True Girlz silver jewelry, 2 25-game travel packs. (Total approx. retail value: $216.00). 25 First Prizes: One copy of Mary-Kate and Ashley Olsen's newest home video, "Passport to Paris" from Warner Home Videos (approx. retail value: $20.00 each).

The sweepstakes is open to legal residents of the U.S. (excluding Puerto Rico) and Canada (excluding Quebec) ages 6-10 as of 4/30/00. Proof of age is required to claim prize. Prizes will be awarded to the winner's parent or legal guardian. Void wherever prohibited or restricted by law. All federal, state and local laws apply. Simon & Schuster, Inc., Parachute Publishing, Warner Bros. and their respective officers, directors, shareholders, employees, suppliers, parent companies, subsidiaries, affiliates, agencies, sponsors, participating retailers, and persons connected with the use, marketing or conduct of this sweepstakes are not eligible. Family members living in the same household as any of the individuals referred to in the preceding sentence are not eligible.

One prize per person or household. Prizes are not transferable and may not be substituted except by sponsors, in the event of prize unavailability, in which case a prize of equal or greater value will be awarded. All prizes will be awarded. The odds of winning a prize depend upon the number of eligible entries received.

Full House™

Sisters

If a winner is a Canadian resident, then he/she must correctly answer a skill-based question administered by mail.

All expenses on receipt and use of prize including federal, state and local taxes are the sole responsibility of the winners. Winners' parents or legal guardians may be required to execute and return an Affidavit of Eligibility and Publicity Release and all other legal documents which the sweepstakes sponsors may require (including a W-9 tax form) within 15 days of attempted notification or an alternate winner will be selected.

Winners or winners' parents or legal guardians on winners' behalf agree to allow use of winners' names, photographs, likenesses, and entries for any advertising, promotion and publicity purposes without further compensation to or permission from the entrants, except where prohibited by law.

Winners and winners' parents or legal guardians agree that Simon & Schuster, Inc., Parachute Publishing and Warner Bros. and their respective officers, directors, shareholders, employees, suppliers, parent companies, subsidiaries, affiliates, agencies, sponsors, participating retailers, and persons connected with the use, marketing or conduct of this sweepstakes, shall have no responsibility or liability for injuries, losses or damages of any kind in connection with the collection, acceptance or use of the prizes awarded herein, or from participation in this promotion.

By participating in this sweepstakes, entrants agree to be bound by these rules and the decisions of the judges and sweepstakes sponsors, which are final in all matters relating to the sweepstakes. Failure to comply with the Official Rules may result in a disqualification of your entry and prohibition of any further participation in this sweepstakes.

The first names the of the winners will be posted at SimonSays.com or the first names of the winners may be obtained by sending a stamped, self-addressed envelope after 5/31/00 to Prize Winners, Pocket Books "Full House Sisters Sweepstakes," 1230 Avenue of the Americas, 13th Floor, NY, NY 10020.